PROMISE
to

JESSICA WOOD

This book is a work of fiction. Names, characters, places, and incidents either are the product of the author's imagination or are used fictitiously. Any resemblance to actual persons, living or dead, events, or locales is entirely coincidental.

Copyright © 2015 by Jessica Wood

All rights reserved. Except as permitted under the U.S. Copyright Act of 1976, no part of this book may be reproduced, scanned, distributed, or transmitted in any form or by any means, or stored in a database or retrieval system, without the prior written permission of the author.

ISBN-13: 978-1507877432

ISBN-10: 1507877439

First Edition: February 2015

Also by Jessica Wood

Emma's Story Series

- *A Night to Forget* – Book One
- *The Day to Remember* – Book Two
- *Emma's Story* Box Set – Contains Book One & Book Two

The Heartbreaker Series

This is an *Emma's Story* spin-off series featuring Damian Castillo, a supporting character in *The Day to Remember*. This is a standalone series and does not need to be read with *Emma's Story* series.

- *Damian* – Book One
- *The Heartbreaker* – Prequel Novella to *DAMIAN* – can be read before or after *Damian*.
- *Taming Damian* – Book Two

- *The Heartbreaker Box Set* – Contains all three books.

The Chase Series

This is a standalone series with cameo appearances from Damian Castillo (*The Heartbreaker series*).

- *The Chase, Vol. 1*
- *The Chase, Vol. 2*
- *The Chase, Vol. 3*
- *The Chase, Vol. 4*
- *The Chase: The Complete Series Box Set* – Contains All Four Volumes

Oblivion

This is a standalone full-length book unrelated to other series by Jessica Wood.

- *Oblivion*

Promises Series

This is a standalone series unrelated to other series by Jessica Wood.

Promise to Marry – Book One

Promise to Keep – Book Two

Promise of Forever – Book Three

PROMISE to Keep

"Forgiveness is me giving up my right to hurt you for hurting me."

Anonymous

Prologue

Chloe

Jackson Pierce. The man I loved. The man I betrayed. The man who hated me.

But he had every right to hate me as much as he did. The secret I'd kept from him was unforgivable, and the untimely way he'd discovered that secret had only strengthened the seed of that hatred, allowing that emotion to deeply root itself inside of him.

But no matter how much he hated me, there would always be someone else who hated me even more. Myself.

For as long as I could remember, my life hadn't been a perfect one. It'd been the opposite of perfect. Things were never black and white, but more gradients of gray—and many ugly fucking grays. When I'd met Jackson, he had become the one part of my life that had been different—the one part of my life that'd been perfect and uncomplicated. The one part of my life that'd made me happy.

But I hadn't expected to ever meet someone like Jackson. I'd grown up thinking that I didn't deserve much happiness—I had no idea what happiness really felt like. So I hadn't allowed myself to believe I deserved a person like him to care for me. I hadn't dared to wish for anything as good as him to happen in my life. Subconsciously, I'd always kept him in the friend-zone, kept him at a safe distance for fear that if I gave in to my feelings for him, I'd somehow inevitably lose him.

In a way, that was exactly what had happened in college. I'd started to imagine the possibilities of something beyond our friendship. And it was then that I'd lost him.

A series of events had led me down a dark path, and I ended up doing something unforgivable. I'd tried to convince myself that it'd only been sex, but I knew deep down that it'd felt wrong, almost forbidden. I'd wanted to tell Jackson everything as soon as it'd happened, but fate had other plans in mind and intervened. And then somehow along the way, I'd somehow convinced myself that he didn't need to know—that he didn't deserve to know. And over time, as it'd become harder and harder to get up the courage to tell him about that part of my life, it'd become easier and easier to compartmentalize my two separate lives. And for over a year, I'd been both the girl Jackson knew as his best friend and the escort he was a stranger to.

It was the one big secret I'd ever kept from Jackson. But like many big secrets, they always had a way of revealing themselves.

And this one had. In possibly the worst way imaginable. My big secret ended up being the thing that tore us apart and ended our friendship.

But how had I fallen down that rabbit hole? And how had I not realized that my actions would inevitably hurt the one person who'd been there for me all these years?

I could try to blame fate or life, but the truth was no one forced me into these choices. I was a flawed person, broken in many ways. It had been my decision and I chose to go down that path.

But I also hadn't sought out the choices I'd made. I hadn't wanted to be an escort. It was one of the hardest decisions I'd ever had to make. And there was a reason for this decision—maybe not a perfect one, in hindsight, but during that moment in time, when push came to shove, when the lives of the people

I cared about the most were on the line, and when time was running out, that was when my decision to be an escort seemed like the *only* option.

But was it worth the betrayal, the disgust, and the hurt that filled Jackson's eyes that day when he'd discovered my secret in the way he did?

No.

No matter how much time had distanced me from that moment—the lowest of my lows—the look on his face when I'd removed my blindfold and saw that it was him had been forever etched into my memory. And every time that memory flashed in my mind, I found it hard to breathe as I felt all the regret and anguish flood back to me, taking me back to that moment.

Maybe I deserved losing Jackson for what I'd done. I had thought that myself many times over. I never even thought I'd deserved him in my life to begin with. But as unrealistic as it was for me to think he'd ever forgive me, a part of me wasn't able to let go of the desperate hope that somehow, by some miracle, he would. And I knew deep down that as long as my heart continued to beat, it couldn't escape the hold he had on me, it couldn't escape the truth I'd tried to ignore. Jackson was a part of me, forever and always.

Chapter One

Present Day

Thirty Years Old

Jackson

Chloe Sinclair. The woman I hated. The woman who'd hurt me in the worst way possible. The woman who I tried so hard to forget over the last nine years.

Since the night I'd stormed out of her apartment nine years ago, I thought I'd never see her again. But when I received the wedding invitation from our mutual high school friend Clara, I knew that I was wrong.

I initially planned on skipping the wedding so I didn't have to see Chloe, but the more I thought about it, the more I realized that in order to really move on with my life, I had to move on from her. Hating her, purposely avoiding her, and allowing her to be the deciding factor in whether or not I attended a friend's wedding didn't feel like actions of someone who'd moved on. I knew I had to go to the wedding and face the situation head on.

But as the weekend of the wedding approached, I realized that I wasn't sure how I felt about seeing her again. I knew a part of me still hated her. I knew our friendship could never be repaired and put back together. But, as much as I wanted to deny it, I also knew that a part of me felt an excited anticipation at seeing her again.

When I arrived in our hometown days before the wedding, the memories of our childhood and friendship were everywhere and unavoidable. As the images of our past came flooding back to me, I was reminded that there was a time when I'd loved her.

If I was completely honest, I think I fell in love with her since as early as first grade. I could still remember that hot summer day when she'd moved in next door. I'd called her Pippi Longstocking and she'd called me a "big meanie," and those had been our first words to one another. I remember thinking that she was the prettiest girl I'd ever seen, and this was during an age when I didn't like girls. In fact, I'd thought girls were really annoying because they giggled about everything and talked too much.

But she had been different from the other girls in school. She hadn't giggled or talked too much. And she had even loved watching *Teenage Mutant Ninja Turtles* almost as much as I had. Before her, I hadn't known any girl who even watched it, let alone loved watching it.

So it wasn't surprising that we quickly became best friends. And from pretty early on, I think I'd wanted us to be something more. But I was young and didn't really understand what it was that I'd been feeling or what it was that I'd wanted more of between us. All I knew then was that I'd wanted to be the most important person in her life, because she was somehow the most important person in mine.

When we were thirteen, she'd lost her mom, and I think it wasn't until then that I'd realized how much I'd cared about her. Watching her in so much pain while pretending to be okay was more than I'd been able to bear. Even though I couldn't take away her pain, I had wanted to make sure she knew that I was going to be there for her. That was when I'd promised her that she'd never have to be alone, and that was when we made our pact to marry each other if we were both single when we turned thirty. That was when we shared our first kiss—my first kiss.

After that first kiss, it became clear to me that I'd wanted more out of our friendship. But because her mom's death had been so recent, I'd decided it wasn't the right time to tell her how I'd felt. I knew that being there for her as her friend was more important. And as time passed, it had become harder to tell her how I felt. I'd been scared that if I told her how I felt and she hadn't felt the same way, things would become awkward and it'd jeopardize our friendship.

So I chickened out and never did tell her how I truly felt.

As I thought back to our childhood together and how close we'd been, I wondered if I was ready to finally face her at the wedding. But I got my answer a day early when I unexpectedly bumped into her during my early morning jog around the neighborhood.

"Hi," she said casually with a bright smile as our eyes met.

"Hey." My voice was flat in contrast to hers. My chest tightened at the sight of her. She was more beautiful than my clearest memories of her. But I couldn't return her smile.

"How are you?" she asked me cheerfully. "Can you believe how long it's been since we've seen each other?"

"Right."

"Nine years, but who's counting?" she continued with a laugh.

I stared at her, unable to respond, let alone laugh. How can she stand there and laugh? How can she pretend like there wasn't a reason why we haven't seen each other?

I realized then that I wasn't ready for this. Suddenly all the images and emotions from the last time I'd seen her came rushing back and consumed my every thought.

It was nine years ago during our junior year of college. We were attending different colleges, six hours away from each other. Our friendship had remained strong, and my feelings for her had never changed. But for one reason or another, I'd never let it show that I'd liked her in that way. In fact, there'd been times I'd encouraged her to go out with men and have some fun. Maybe I was a masochist when it came to love?

But it hadn't been until our junior year that our friendship changed. I'd started to notice that she seemed jealous over the girls I'd been seeing, something I hadn't noticed before. Pretty quickly, our phone calls became more flirtatious and sexually charged. It wasn't until then that I'd finally gotten up the courage to tell her how I'd felt. I decided to visit her. She'd visited me a few times in college, but somehow, I'd never taken the trip down to visit her. When I'd told her I wanted to visit for the weekend, I could tell she was beyond thrilled about it, which only fueled my anticipation for our weekend together. I knew it'd be a weekend I wouldn't forget. It'd be a weekend that'd forever change our relationship.

Because my only Friday class had been cancelled that week, I'd decided to surprise Chloe and take an earlier train down to see her. But when I got off the train in Philadelphia, I realized that I should probably have told her I was coming over and tried to call her.

Her phone had been turned off, so I'd decided to text her in case she was in class and told her I'd stop by her apartment to see if she was there. What I hadn't expected was what happened next.

She had been home, and she'd been waiting in her bedroom, blind-folded and with nothing on but a sexy, red-laced lingerie number that'd left nothing to the imagination. She'd invited me into her bed, and that was the first time I'd made love to her. I'd remembered how soft and deliciously sweet she'd been on my tongue as I'd explored her with abandonment. I'd remembered the sheer ecstasy of finally being inside of her as she cried out, begging for more, urging me to go even deeper and harder inside her. I'd been more than willing to oblige. And I'd remembered as I reached the peak of my climax, a thought as clear as day crossed my mind: *She feels the same about me as I do about her. Why wait until we're thirty? I want her to be mine now.*

But I couldn't have been more wrong. It'd been only seconds after I had had that thought that my world came crashing down on me when Chloe said,

"That was incredible! Especially that thing you did at the very end. How come you've never done that before?" I'd felt my chest constrict as I realized that it hadn't been me she thought was making love to her. She'd been expecting someone else. As my body reeled from the shock of the truth, a man—the one she'd been expecting instead of me—came barging through the door, and suddenly all the air was sucked out of the room as I'd found myself face-to-face with the last person I'd expected to see. *My own father.*

For one split all-consuming second after I'd seen that it'd been my father she'd been waiting on and not me, rage had filled me to my very core and all I wanted to do was grab this stranger that was in my father's body and beat the living shit out of him. But I hadn't acted on that rage against that man. Instead I'd taken it all out on Chloe, and the minutes that followed have since become a blur in my memories. I remembered pushing my way out of her apartment as she'd tried so desperately to stop me, to tell me why she'd done what she'd done. But I couldn't see the tears that were falling down her cheeks and I didn't care to hear anything that she had had to say. All I had been able to hear was the ringing in my ears as the rage gripped my every thought, and all I'd wanted to do was get as far away from her as I could.

So I'd been right. That weekend was one I'd never forget. That weekend did forever change my relationship with Chloe. But what I hadn't expected was how *wrong* I'd been in how things would change. It'd turned out that the first time I'd made love to the girl who'd possessed my heart turned out to be the first time I'd ever hated her. It was the first time she'd ever hurt me. It was the first time I'd wanted nothing to do with her.

Now, nine years later, as we stood in front of each other for the first time since that night, I realized that I hadn't gotten over what'd happened years ago. I hadn't forgiven her for sleeping with my father, and I wasn't ready to forgive her. When I looked at her, all I could think about was the fact that she hadn't made love to me or had those same feelings for me that I'd had for her. All I could think about was the fact that of all the guys she could have slept with instead of me, she'd chosen to sleep with my father.

So the more she tried to apologize and beg for my forgiveness that morning and then at the wedding reception the next day, the colder I was toward her. I thought that there was nothing she could say that would push away the hatred I had for her. But I was wrong. At the wedding reception, I'd asked her in spite why she'd insisted on sitting right next to me when our table had eight other empty seats. She'd said: *"Because you won't talk to me, you won't look at me, and you won't forgive me. Because I miss you. Very much. And every single day. Because for the last nine years, there hasn't been a single day that I didn't hate myself for hurting you. Because I lost my first and only best friend in the world, the man I recently realized that I love and want a life with. And because if I didn't at least tell you all this when I had the chance, there'd be another reason to hate myself every day."*

Her words caught me by surprise. I knew they were genuine and I felt my will power to stay angry at her begin to crumble. As I took in her words, I wasn't able to react or respond. Everything she just confessed to feeling were feelings I'd had for her, and I'd longed to hear her tell me she loved me and wanted a future with me. But as I sat there, I was torn between my hatred and my love for the best friend I'd known since I was eight—the girl I had made a pact to marry.

But before I had time to process my own thoughts, to figure out if my feelings for her were enough to overcome the hatred inside me, I heard her get up and rush out of the reception hall. I resisted the urge to run after her. I wasn't sure I was ready to talk to her, to admit to her my feelings, to admit how much she'd hurt me, to admit to myself that I still cared for her. But as I sat there alone, I felt my resolve start to waver. As much as I wanted to hold on to the anger that tainted my memories of her, I knew I had to see her. I wasn't sure what I'd say to her, or if I'd even say anything at all. But her last words echoed in my mind, *"…if I didn't at least tell you all this when I had the chance, there'd be another reason to hate myself every day."* I realized that this could be the last time I'd ever see her, and I knew that this wasn't the way I wanted our last conversation to end.

Without giving it another thought, I got up quickly and went after her. I caught a glimpse of her standing outside talking on the phone. Just as I pushed through the front door leading out of the building, I saw Chloe faint and fall lifelessly onto the ground.

Chapter Two

Present Day

Thirty Years Old

Chloe

"My dad?" he spat out the words as he turned from his father to look at me. I saw the pure shock, disgust, and hurt painted across his face and echoed in his ice-cold glare, and I felt myself recoil in response. I'd never seen him look at me like this before—his eyes were devoid of that warmth that I'd grown used to. He looked at me like I was a complete stranger to him.

"Jax, I can explain—" I started.

"—Explain?" He cut me off, his voice cold and laced with venom. "How exactly are you going to explain this?" he demanded, daring me to answer him. "Are you going to try to convince me that you knew it was me that was fucking you just now? Are you going to try to convince me that you had no idea that my dad was going to stop by with a hard Viagra dick? Are you going to try to convince me that you haven't fucked my dad before?" I could hear the mix of disgust and hurt in his questions. "Or…are you going to tell me the truth?"

The betrayal and hurt in his eyes made it hard to breathe. "I…" I was at a loss for words and tried to think through the panic that paralyzed my body and the rapid beating of my heart. "I wanted to tell you, Jax. I don't want to lie to you—"

His crazed laughter cut me as he grabbed his clothes that were scattered around the floor. "You don't want to lie to me? That's fresh." He snorted. "I really find that hard to believe."

"Jackson, we're all adults here, and no one's been lying to you," John, Jackson's father, finally spoke.

"Are you fucking serious, Dad? Not lying to me?" By now, Jackson had put on all his clothes and started to head for the bedroom door.

"We weren't. Chloe and I are consensual adults and you guys are just friends. Nothing we're doing is wrong."

I felt sick and my insides twisted with anxiety as I heard John trying to justify what we'd been doing. I knew he was making things worse, but I couldn't think of anything to say that could possibly make it better.

"Please, Jax. Can we please talk about this alone? I want to explain everything to you," I pleaded as I followed him to the bedroom door.

"There's nothing to talk about, Chloe."

I winced at hearing him call me by my full name instead of his nickname for me. "I'm so sorry, Jax. I didn't mean for you to find out this way. I really wanted to tell you." I wasn't sure what to say. How could I blurt out the fact that I was an escort at this point? How could I tell him that his father wasn't the only man I'd slept with regularly? I knew it would only make matters worse when he was so consumed with rage. "Please can we sit down and talk about this?"

"I've heard enough!" He pushed back his father and walked through the living room toward the front door.

"Jax! Please!" I raced after him, panic radiating through me, and I knew I couldn't let him leave like this. "I needed the money!" I heard myself blurt out before I could think through what I'd wanted to say.

He whipped around, his eyes ablaze in a crazed frenzy. "You needed money? How come you didn't come to me? I could've given you some money if you needed help! How come you went to my dad? Is he your sugar daddy? Was this why my parents got a divorce two years ago?"

"No, that had nothing to do with me." I ran to him and reached for his hands, trying to do anything that would keep him from walking out the front door, trying to convince him to stay long enough to hear me out.

"She's right, son. Your mom and I was going through our divorce a year before anything happened between Chloe and I," John offered as he walked into the living room from the bedroom.

I cringed as I saw Jackson doing the math in his head before he looked at me, his face twisted in revulsion. "You've been fucking my dad for a year?" He looked at me in a way that frightened me, like he was looking at a complete stranger he couldn't understand.

"I…" I bowed my head and nodded in shame, unable to meet his eyes. I knew there was nothing I could say to make the situation better. "I'm really sorry.

I really am," I whispered. "I had my reasons, if you'll just let me explain…"

But he didn't seem to hear a word I'd said. "You fucking whore!" His words cut through me like a sharp blade, causing me to look up and meet his gaze. I saw the sheer rage in his cold, piercing green eyes, and I knew then that I'd lost him.

"I'm sorry, Jax. Please let me explain," I pleaded again as tears began to stream down my face. I could hear the desperation in my own voice.

To my surprise, he took a step toward me and looked me square in the eyes as he leaned in. With our faces only inches apart, he said through gritted teeth, "Sorry isn't enough to repair this. You fucked this all up. I don't want to see or hear from you ever again. As far as I'm concerned, the Chloe that was my best friend for the past fourteen years is dead to me."

Before I could respond, he turned away from me and stormed out of my apartment.

"Jax…" I mumbled as I struggled to open my eyes against the weight of my heavy eyelids. As the hazy veil of sleep lifted from my consciousness, I wished desperately that what I'd just dreamed about was merely a dream.

But I knew it wasn't. I knew every vivid second of that dream had happened.

When I finally opened my eyes, I realized I was lying in a hospital bed. As I began to sit up, I noticed an IV hooked to my arm, and I tried to think back to the last thing I could remember before waking up here.

Aunt Betty!

I instantly bolted straight up as I remembered my call with Uncle Tom. As I tried to pull the IV out of my arm, a nurse walked into the room.

"Ms. Sinclair, it's good to see you awake."

"What happened to me?" I looked at the IV. "What is this?"

"It's nothing to worry about. You fainted a few hours ago and were brought in. It looked like you had quite a few drinks tonight on an empty stomach and you were dehydrated. So the IV bag just contains some water and sugar to help rehydrate you. How are you feeling?"

"Nurse, is there a Betty Kline here at this hospital?" I asked with a rush of urgency as I ignored her question. "She's my aunt, and my uncle had called me earlier and told me they were at the hospital."

The nurse flashed me a small understanding smile. "Don't worry, Ms. Sinclair. Your aunt will be fine. Your uncle stopped by earlier when you were still asleep. They're just down the hall."

"Can I go see her?" I looked at the IV and then back at her.

"Sure. Let me get that for you." She reached over and helped me remove the IV from my arm. "How are you feeling?"

"I'm okay." Then a thought came to me as I got out of the hospital bed. "How did I get here?"

"I think a young man brought you in."

My face lit up at her answer, and I wondered if the young man was Jackson. "Really?" I paused, almost afraid to ask further. "Is…is he still here?"

"I don't think so," she responded nonchalantly. "I think he just dropped you off and talked to your uncle briefly before leaving."

"Oh." I tried to hide the disappointment from my response and busied myself as I readjusted the hospital gown around my body. "Can you tell me what room my aunt's in?"

"No problem. Let me walk you there."

Moments later, I was hugging Uncle Tom right outside of Aunt Betty's hospital room.

"Are you okay, Chloe? I was worried about you."

"Yes, I'm fine. I'm sorry to have scared you. What happened to Aunt Betty? Will she be okay?" I looked over his shoulder at Aunt Betty, who was asleep on the hospital bed.

"Don't worry. The doctor said she'll be okay. She fell off a step stool while getting something in the pantry. I think her hip might have momentarily given out on her. You know her hip hasn't been the same since that car accident."

"Yeah." I nodded solemnly.

"But she was lucky. The doctor said he doesn't think she sustained any severe injuries, so she should be free to leave in a few days."

I let out a sigh of relief. "That's good."

"Honey, are you really feeling okay?" Uncle Tom studied me with concern.

"Yeah, I'm fine. Why?"

"Well, Jackson brought you in here because you'd fainted at the wedding reception."

"Oh." Hearing Jackson's name said out loud caused my stomach to flip with anxiety. "Did you talk to him or see him?" I looked at Uncle Tom hopefully. I felt pathetic for being overly eager, but when it came to Jackson, I was like a dry sponge, desperate to soak up any information I could that involved him.

"Yeah. I spoke to him when you had fainted during our call. He picked up the phone and that's how he knew where your aunt and I were. So he drove you to this hospital and the nurses put you on an IV as a precautionary measure. I talked to him briefly before he left."

"Really? What did you guys talk about?"

"Nothing really. He stopped by to check on Betty, and then headed home."

"Oh. Okay." I wanted to ask if Jackson mentioned anything about me, but I had a feeling I wouldn't like the answer so held my tongue.

"Honey, it's getting late. Why don't you take my car and head on home and get some rest?"

"But what about you?"

"The nurses brought out a cot for me, so I'm going to stay with Betty in her room."

I looked back inside the hospital room, this time noticing the small cot flush against the far wall. I also saw a bench against the window. "I don't feel like being alone tonight. Is it okay if I stay with you guys in the room tonight? I can take that bench by the window."

"Of course, honey." Uncle Tom gave me an understanding smile before we both headed into Aunt Betty's hospital room.

***

I woke up the next morning with a groan as my hand reached up to massage the crick in my neck.

"Good morning, sweetie."

I smiled as soon as I heard her voice. "Good morning, Aunt Betty. How are you feeling?" I walked over to her bed.

She smiled at me. "Not bad with all things considered."

"Where's Uncle Tom?" I asked as my eyes glanced at the empty cot.

"He went down to the cafeteria to get some coffee and breakfast."

"Gotcha." My stomach growled at the mention of food, reminding me that I hadn't had any food since early yesterday.

"Honey, are you feeling okay? I heard you fainted last night."

I gave her a small reassuring smile. "I'm fine. Really."

She frowned and pressed her lips together. "Are you sure?"

I nodded. "Yeah."

"Honey…" she began. From the hesitation in her voice, I knew she had something on her mind.

"What is it, Aunt Betty?" I met her concerned gaze and felt my body prick with anxiety.

"Is everything okay with you and Jackson?"

I was blindsided by her question, leaving me momentarily speechless.

"Honey, if there's anything troubling you, you know I'm here to listen, right? You can tell me anything…"

"Why do you ask?" I tried to sound casual as I turned my face away from her and blinked away the tears that welled up in my eyes.

I heard her sigh. "Chloe, I watched you grow up. I can tell when something's bothering you. I've known that something is wrong for quite some time now, but I didn't want to ask. I know you like to process things in your own way. But since you've been back home this week, I can tell that whatever's bothering you hasn't gone away. I get the sense that it has something to do with Jackson."

"Why do you think that?" I asked hesitantly as I turned back to meet her gaze.

She flashed me an understanding smile. "Because I watched Jackson grow up too, and I want to believe that I know him almost as well as I know you. And when I talked to him last night, I could tell there was something wrong. He was distant and didn't really mention your name, which is very odd for him."

It was then that I started to unravel and realized that I wasn't able to keep my secret from Aunt Betty any longer. My need to talk to someone about everything that'd happened—everything I'd bottled up inside for the past nine years—overwhelmed me, and I knew that I'd go crazy if I didn't let it all out.

So I finally gave in to the need, and I told her everything that'd happened. I felt waves of shame, regret, embarrassment and self-loathing as I heard myself recount everything I'd done out loud. I'd expected Aunt Betty to look at me with disappointment and disgust, but to my surprise, she had tears in her eyes as she listened in silence to my story.

After I told her everything, I felt as if a weight had been lifted from my shoulders. It felt liberating to finally tell someone about what had happened.

Shortly after our conversation, Uncle Tom returned from the cafeteria. Feeling hungry and disheveled, I was craving some food and a nice, hot shower. I gave Aunt Betty and Uncle Tom each a kiss goodbye before heading out of the hospital room.

As I walked to the side entrance of the hospital toward the parking lot where Uncle Tom said he'd parked his car, I suddenly gasped and stopped mid-step when I saw him. There, less than fifty yards away, was Jackson walking toward me with a bouquet of flowers in his hands.

Chapter Three

Present Day

Thirty Years Old

Jackson

I saw her before she'd spotted me. My chest instantly tightened at the sight of her and the competing feelings I felt for her fought for their control inside me.

She stopped in her tracks the moment she saw me. Then she started walking toward me, causing me to draw in a deep breath. I was surprised that even after everything I'd said to her and how cold I'd treated her, she still wanted to talk to me and even approached me with a smile on her face.

"Hi," she said in a low, breathy voice when she stopped in front of me. "Thank you for getting me to the hospital last night."

"Yeah. No problem." My voice was flat and distant.

Her smile fell slightly. "Are those...?" She didn't finish her question as she looked tentatively between me and the flowers in my hand.

"They're for Aunt Betty," I explained.

"Oh." Her expression changed for a moment, but her smile remained curled on her lips. "They're beautiful tulips. She will love those."

I couldn't help feeling bad when I remembered that tulips were Chloe's favorite flowers and wondered if she had thought that I was here to see her and these tulips were for her. A dull ache that I'd ignored for so long ran through me as I saw the look in her eyes. In that instant I felt a longing for her. I missed her.

"Yeah, I wanted to stop by to see that she's okay. She was always there to care for me when we were growing up." I felt compelled to explain myself. "It's the least I can do to thank her for all the lunch money she'd saved me by packing me those school lunches." I gave a light chuckle, hoping to lighten the tension I felt between us.

"That's sweet of you. I know that'll mean a lot to her." Her voice was friendly, but in that overly polite way.

A part of me wanted to say something that would make her feel better, but I didn't. As I looked at her, I realized that I wasn't ready to forgive her. Even though I missed her, I still couldn't understand how she had done something so unforgivable years ago. How could I forgive her when I couldn't understand her? Or when I felt like I didn't know her at all?

"Well, I should go see her, then," I ended up saying instead. "Bye." I felt my stomach clench in guilt as I forced my legs to move and walk past her.

"Wait." She turned and took a step toward me.

I stopped but didn't turn around to meet her gaze.

"Can we talk?" There was a crack in her voice that tore at my insides.

We stood there in silence for what seemed like forever before I finally spoke. "I'm not sure I'm ready for that," I said honestly.

"I'm sorry for what I did to you. I…"

"It's all in the past. Let's just leave it all in the past and not dwell on it." My jaws tightened as I tried to work through my feelings.

"I called you a few months ago," she blurted out. "I…I wanted to talk to you and tell you everything…I still do."

Emotions whirled inside me, and I wasn't sure I wanted to hear about the feelings she had for my father or details about their relationship or why it was all okay. I'd heard enough of those reasons from my father the few times we'd spoken to each other after the incident. I didn't need to hear them repeated by the woman who'd broken my heart as well.

"I know you called," I said flatly. I remembered that night clearly. It was around three in the morning when she'd called. In my half-asleep state, I hadn't looked at the caller ID when I'd picked up. But when I didn't hear anything on the other end of the line, I hung up. It wasn't until then that I realized who had just called.

"You did?" I heard the surprise in her voice. "How come you hadn't mentioned that?"

I didn't turn to look at her. I wasn't sure I could. "You called in the middle of the night and you didn't say anything when I had answered. So I knew you must have called me by mistake. I didn't think it was anything I needed to mention again."

"Oh."

"I should go see your aunt now. My train back to New York leaves in a few hours."

"You're leaving already?" I could hear the surprise and disappointment in her voice. "I thought maybe we could…"

There was a part of me that wanted to stay and talk to her, but there was a bigger, and stronger, part of me that wasn't ready to face her. "Yeah. I need to head back. The wedding's over so there's nothing here that I need to stay for." I felt awful the second I heard the words come out of my mouth.

"Right." Her voice was strained and then she paused before continuing quickly. "Well, enjoy your visit. I gotta go."

I turned around toward her, immediately regretting my words. But when I did, she was already running halfway down the corridor toward the parking garage.

I thought about chasing after her, but I stopped myself. What would I say? What would it accomplish? So instead, I turned back around and headed to Aunt Betty's hospital room. I tried to push away the feeling, but a heaviness took residence inside my chest as I imagined Chloe running away from me with tears streaming down her face.

***

"Jackson, it's great to see you again." Aunt Betty beamed at me as I walked in to her hospital room.

"Hi, Aunt Betty. How are you feeling?" I leaned over and kissed her on the cheek.

"Not bad. They gave me something for the hip, so I'm feeling better. Luckily I didn't fracture anything so I won't need any surgery, but they want to keep me here for the next day or so to run some more tests."

"That's good to hear." I felt relieved by the news. Aunt Betty was such a kind person, and she'd gone through so much since I'd known her. I didn't want to see her in pain. "Oh, and this is for you. I hope it'll brighten up your day a bit." I handed her the bouquet of tulips.

"Oh, you're such a sweet child, Jackson. They're beautiful." She took the flowers and smiled at them. "But are you sure you got these for me?" she asked as she looked up at me with a curious smile on her face.

"What do you mean?" I asked, feeling a sense of unease by her question.

She grinned at me. "You know that tulips are Chloe's favorite. You used to get them for her when she needed cheering up."

"I actually forgot about that when I'd gotten these," I admitted as a wave of guilt washed over me. I wasn't sure why I'd picked up the bouquet of tulips among the various flowers that'd been available that morning at the floral shop. But when I saw the tulips, I'd smiled and gravitated toward them. *Was I thinking about her without even knowing it?*

Aunt Betty didn't respond for a moment, but simply studied me. "Jackson, can I be frank?"

"Sure. Of course." I felt my body stiffen and braced myself for whatever she planned on saying.

"Is everything okay between you and Chloe?"

I swallowed uncomfortably when I heard her unexpected and direct question, and I wasn't sure how to respond.

"Why do you ask that?" I finally asked, trying to stall for time.

There was a brief moment of silence and I could tell she was considering something. When she finally spoke, I noticed her voice changed and became more serious. "Jackson, Chloe told me that you guys aren't friends anymore."

"She did?" I felt the blood drain from my face. I wasn't sure why, but I'd never told anyone about what happened between me and Chloe nine years ago. I'd never once admitted to anyone, but Chloe, that we were no longer friends and that I hated her. But now hearing Aunt Betty say those words, it felt like a punch in the stomach. In a way, it made what happened that night years ago more of a reality.

Aunt Betty nodded. "She told me everything." She paused. "I can't imagine how you must have felt that day when you found out, and I know you might not want to hear this, but believe me when I say that Chloe didn't want you to find out that way. I think she felt so ashamed by what was going on that it got to a point where she didn't want you to know at all."

Shock flooded through my system as I took in her words. I didn't know if I wanted to talk about what had happened with Aunt Betty, but seeing her calm demeanor as she tried to justify Chloe's actions caused me to question what she knew. *How could she not be upset by the fact that Chloe had a relationship with my father?*

"I'm not sure what to say." I felt the need to defend myself. "If you want me to forgive her, I'm not sure I can do that. I think that's asking a bit too much."

She gave a solemn nod of her head. "I know. I understand. I'm not asking you to forgive her, Jackson.

I know it's none of my business and this is something between you and Chloe. All I am asking is for you to try to hear her out and maybe keep an open mind."

"An open mind? What do you mean by that?" I searched her face for answers. "What do you know that I don't?"

She frowned and I noticed how sad she was at that moment. "I shouldn't be the one to tell you everything that she went through. I think you should hear it directly from her. But I have a feeling that if I don't say anything, you will continue to be mad at her without wanting to knowing why."

I wanted to tell her that she was wrong, that I knew the reason I was mad at her. I wanted to tell her that Chloe made it clear to me that night that she had feelings for my father. I wanted to tell her that that Chloe had picked him over me, that Chloe had been romantically involved with my father without ever thinking to tell me, without ever considering my feelings. But something stopped me from voicing my thoughts, as if saying them out loud would bring back all the pain I'd felt the day I'd found out about their relationship. So instead of voicing my disagreement, I decided to listen to what Aunt Betty had to say.

"So what I will tell you is this: she wasn't an escort for herself, or because she wanted to. It was the opposite. It was the most selfless thing anyone could do, and she did it to help me and Tom." Her words ended in a whisper as tears fell down her face.

I stared at her in complete silence, unable to comprehend what she'd just said.

"Escort? What? Did you just say she was an escort?" I finally managed to ask. My mind whirled with a million thoughts but I couldn't seem to grasp onto anything specific to focus on. *I must have misunderstood what she'd just said.*

"You didn't know that?" She looked at me in surprise. "Oh my, I…"

I shook my head. "No. She didn't tell me. She just said she needed money—" I paused, feeling another pang of guilt wash over me. "—but then I stopped listening to her." I felt a lump develop in my throat. "How come she didn't ask me for help though? I could have given her the money. Why did she have to turn to something as debasing as selling her own body?" Then another thought flashed through my mind. "Was my father a *client*?" I asked incredulously, unable to believe that any of this could be even remotely true.

Aunt Betty looked away. "You should really talk to her about this. I feel like I've already said too much." She paused. "But to answer one of your questions, I will say that she needed a lot of money at that time—more than you could have helped her out with."

"But that's still not a good reason to turn to something like escorting!" I heard my voice rise as a mixture of anger, confusion, and guilt consumed me. "Why didn't she at least ask for help?"

She sighed. "You've known Chloe for most of your life. You know she has a lot of pride and doesn't want to ask for help. Before she lived with us, she'd learned to take care of herself and face her problems alone. I don't think that instinct ever left her, even when she moved in with us and we were there to help her. She's always wanted to be independent and be able to solve her problems on her own. Even with me and Tom, she always resisted our help and didn't want to depend on us. I think one of her biggest fears is to be a burden on someone else." She let out a deep sigh. "I think with the way her mother left her, she was always scared that she'd become a burden to us and make our lives harder, and she didn't want to live with the guilt if something bad were to happen to us as a result."

Everything Aunt Betty had said was true. I'd noticed this about Chloe as well. But it still didn't take away the hatred I'd felt for Chloe for hurting me. "But I'm—I *was* her best friend. She should have at least told me she was about to become an escort! Why did she keep it from me? And why had she been sleeping with my father of all people?" An image of that night flashed before my eyes, and I felt all the anger and pain return. "How can I forgive her for something like that? How can you ask me to have an open mind when she had been sleeping with my own father?"

She nodded as if she understood my frustration and anger. "I know, Jackson. She should have told you about what we were going through after the car accident and why she decided to become an escort. She should have told you about your father. I don't think it was a matter of her not wanting to tell you. I think she had wanted to tell you. And she had planned on telling you as soon as things had happened."

"So why didn't she tell me? She apparently had at least a whole year to do so." I cut her off, frustrated by what I was hearing. How could Aunt Betty possibly believe that Chloe had wanted to tell me everything when she clearly kept it from me for over a year?

Aunt Betty shook her head. "That's something you'll have to ask her. I actually don't know that part. All she had said was that something had caused her to change her mind and she decided not to tell you. But she wouldn't tell me what had changed her mind."

I frowned, dissatisfied with that answer. It wasn't enough for me.

As if reading my mind, Aunt Betty continued. "Just think about it, Jackson. You've known her since she was seven. Do you really believe it's like her to keep something like this from you without an understandable reason? Do you really believe she's the type of person who would intentionally hurt her best friend, the boy she's loved since she was seven?"

Her last words took me by surprise. "She didn't love me then. She never told me."

Aunt Betty gave a light chuckle and shook her head. "Jackson, I know you've loved Chloe for as long as she's loved you. Have you once told her?"

I didn't answer her, but her words stayed with me. As much as I wanted to remain angry with Chloe, I felt the solid fortress of hatred I'd built around my heart for her begin to crack and crumble.

To my surprise, there was also another emotion I'd been feeling that I hadn't expected: relief. Maybe it would have been more natural for me to be upset knowing now that Chloe had been an escort and had slept with men—including my father—for money. But surprisingly, I was more relieved than upset about this. After what had happened, I'd always thought that I'd been played a fool, that I'd been lied to, that her feelings for me had all been a farce. I thought that Chloe wasn't the person I'd thought she was. I thought I didn't know her at all.

But now I wondered if I'd been wrong all along. It was then that it hit me. Since that night nine years ago, I had selfishly built this hatred for her based solely on my own emotions and how she'd hurt me. I'd judged her like a total stranger would have passed judgment on her. I'd somehow discounted the previous fourteen years I'd known her, the fourteen years she'd been my best friend, the previous fourteen years I'd loved her. I'd always thought she'd slept with my father because she didn't have the same feelings I'd had for her, and that rejection had blinded me. I'd made assumptions about her reasons for sleeping with my father without ever once wondering if that was the Chloe I'd known, without ever once giving her a chance to explain her side of the story. In the last nine years I'd hated her, I'd never once wondered if she had a good reason for what she'd done, if her reasons had nothing to do with me and how much she'd hurt me. Instead, I'd only hated her and that hatred bled through every fiber of my being and every part of me that loved her.

When I left the hospital half an hour later, I was riddled with guilt as I let my conversation with Aunt Betty sink in. My mind went back to everything that'd happened in the year leading up to that night I'd made love to Chloe. I remembered Chloe going through some problems after the accident, but I was too involved with my fraternity and college to really pay attention or be there for her. I knew I'd upset her several times, especially the time she'd come to visit me unannounced. But at the time, I didn't think anything of it. Had she tried to tell me, but I'd been too involved with my own life to know? Had she been going through a tough time and I hadn't been there for her?

Aunt Betty was right. She'd been my best friend and I'd known her better than anyone else had. I'd used that night as the reason to convince myself that I hadn't known her at all. But if I'd taken the time to really think things through rationally, I should have known that something hadn't made sense. It wasn't like her to have done what she did without a good reason.

I clenched my fist as I started to feel the anger rise within me. But this time, it wasn't directed at Chloe. It was directed at the situation we were in. I felt feelings of confusion and guilt wash over me—confusion for not knowing what had been wrong with Chloe in college and guilt for not realizing that something had been wrong.

I'd once thought my love for her was unconditional, that I'd love her until my last dying breath. But I realized then that I'd been wrong. My love for her had been juvenile and selfish. I'd never told her how I really felt. And yet, like a coward, I'd slept with other women because I wanted to test her and because I thought she wasn't interested in me. I'd even encouraged her to sleep around herself.

Today, after all these years, I finally realized that the explanation I'd created in my mind for her betrayal may not be the reality. Now I wondered how desperate and low she must have felt to go through with what she had done.

As I drove back home, I felt torn over how I felt about Chloe, the girl who'd been my best friend for most of my life, the girl who I'd loved more than anyone else, the girl who'd broken my heart. Now that I knew there was more to the story than what I knew, could her reasons be enough for me to forgive and forget what'd happened nine years ago? Could I really get over what I'd seen that night? Could my feelings for her ever be as pure and true as they'd been before that night?

I didn't know.

But what I did know was, I had to see her and this time, I had to listen to her side of the story.

Chapter Four

November 2000

Sixteen Years Old

Chloe

I couldn't stop grinning as I stared at the shiny laminated card clutched in my hands. Having a learner's permit didn't just mean I was now able to practice driving behind the wheel of an actual car, it meant I was one step closer to freedom. Jackson had teased me mercilessly when he received his before me and I couldn't wait to show him that he was no better than I was now.

"Bet you'll fail!" he had taunted me over burgers and fries after I told him I was going to the DMV for the exam the next day. "That test is brutal! All trick questions! Most kids don't pass it the first time, but of course I did because you know me, I'm a freaking genius." He flashed me a boyish grin that only further complemented his natural charm.

"Bullshit! You don't scare me," I said as I playfully threw a ketchup-coated fry at him. But the truth was, he had passed his first time.

I stayed up for hours that night memorizing the study guide book in preparation. If he was right and I failed, it would be beyond humiliating, because it meant that he would have bragging rights over me forever, and I knew he wouldn't let me live it down.

When Aunt Betty drove me to the DMV the next morning, I felt queasy and my eyes stung from the little sleep I had gotten the night before. At first, the questions blurred across the page, and I had to blink several times and force myself to concentrate. When the test finally came into focus, I saw that the questions were hard. But thanks to Jackson, I knew almost every answer. When the clerk handed me back my paper, I'd scored a ninety-five percent. I squealed with excitement as I jumped up and down at the counter.

"Very good, young lady. This is the best score I've seen all week." The clerk had said as she directed me to stand behind the white line and smile for the camera. Just a few minutes later, she handed me the card, fresh from the lamination machine. I smiled to myself as my hand touched my still-hot driver's permit.

Pennsylvania

Instruction Permit

Chloe Sinclair

I read each line of the card and felt the butterflies in my stomach turn into the excited pounding of my heart. I'd done it. This was the first step toward being independent and not having to depend on Aunt Betty and Uncle Tom. As grateful as I was for everything they'd provided me since I'd moved in with them eight years ago, I couldn't help but feel like a burden and an extra expense for them before they were able to retire. Their son, Charlie, who was eleven years older than me, supported himself financially. I'd heard Aunt Betty and Uncle Tom talk about their retirement before, and I knew they were trying to save up so that they could retire a few years early. I didn't want to be the reason they couldn't make that happen. I knew my driver's permit was one step closer to my ability to take care of myself.

"Congratulations, honey!" Aunt Betty hugged me right in the lobby of the DMV and I shrugged out of her embrace.

"Not in front of everybody!" I rolled my eyes, feeling embarrassed over the attention. "Can I go to

Jackson's house?" I asked immediately, knowing that he was the first person I wanted to show my new permit to.

"Sure." Aunt Betty smiled.

When we got to the Pierce's home, I waved goodbye to Aunt Betty and made sure she had left before ringing the doorbell. I loved her, but she could be so embarrassing sometimes. There was no doubt that if Jackson or his parents had opened the door before she left, she would have gone on and on to them about how proud she was of me for passing the exam on the first try, and how hard I'd studied for the exam.

Once she had safely rounded the corner, I rang the doorbell and quickly hid the card behind my back, bristling with anticipation. Jackson was going to shit himself when he saw that I had passed the exam on my first try, too.

But to my surprise, his father opened the door. It was rare for him to be home in the middle of the afternoon.

"Hi there, Chloe. It's always a pleasure to see you." He smiled at me and held the door open so I could enter.

"Is Jax home?" I asked, already heading toward his room.

"No, he's not back from football practice yet."

The look of disappointment must have been evident on my face, because he immediately said, "I expect him back soon, though. You're welcome to wait if you don't mind hanging out for a few minutes with an old guy like myself."

"You're not old." I laughed. I remembered when I was younger, I had thought Jackson's father was ancient. But now that I was a little older, I thought he looked like Harrison Ford. There was a similarity in the eyes and the crooked grin. He was funny, kind, and had a certain charm, at least for an older guy. I wondered if

Jackson would be handsome like his dad one day and I smiled, thinking he was already handsome.

"What's behind your back?" he asked and I flushed to suddenly remembering that I'd been planning to surprise Jackson.

"Oh, nothing. Just this," I said and I could feel my cheeks starting to burn. I held out my hand from behind my back and he gently picked up the card and read it. A grin curled the corners of his lips and his eyes flashed with happiness on my behalf.

"Congratulations! That's a big deal getting your learner's permit." He moved toward me as if to hug me like Aunt Betty had done. I felt my heart begin to pound in my chest, mortified at the mere thought of it. But I had panicked for nothing. He was simply reaching out to return the permit to me. As I sighed with relief, a part of me was a little disappointed. Maybe it wouldn't be so bad to be hugged by a man as smart and mature as Mr. Pierce. *That's silly, though.* I quickly shook the thought from my mind.

"Come sit with me and tell me what else is new with you." He plopped comfortably on the couch in their living room and patted the cushion next to him. "I've been working so many hours lately, I never see you kids anymore. Please, tell me how you've been."

I felt bad for Mr. Pierce. He really did work a lot and whenever I saw him, I got the feeling that he was lonely and missed his family. It was obvious he felt bad about not being able to spend more time with Jackson. Unfortunately, Jackson didn't see it that way and complained to me about his dad on the rare instances that he mentioned him. Maybe if I sat and talked to Jackson's father a little about his son, it would help make their relationship closer. It seemed like the least I could do.

"Things are good. Jax and I have almost all the same classes together this year, except for math and P.E. He's doing really great in football; even though he's a freshman, the coach let him play in the last three games. The first time was because several of the regular players were hurt and they needed a linebacker. He did so well, the coach has played him every game since." I could have bragged about Jackson for hours, but his father cut me off with a friendly chuckle.

"That's great about Jackson, but I was asking about you. How have you been, Chloe?"

No one ever really asked me about myself—especially not adults. It was weird, but kind of nice, too. Jackson was lucky to have a good dad; sweet, sensitive, and really caring.

I wanted to respond, but I realized that I didn't really know what to say about myself. I shifted uncomfortably as I tried to think of something to say that didn't sound totally stupid.

Jackson's father tried to break the ice for me, asking casually, "How are your classes?"

"Good, I guess. I've got almost all As, and just a few Bs." I tried not to sound like I was bragging, and added, "Oh, and one D."

It was something I hadn't confessed to anyone else yet, but for some reason I felt comfortable enough to tell Jackson's father. I guess I just wanted to test the waters and see if he would freak out like Uncle Tom would and lecture me on the importance of grades or if he was really as cool as he seemed.

"What subject?" he asked and I could feel the lecture coming on.

"Math." I said, biting my lower lip. "It's algebra and the teacher goes over everything so fast I can't follow him."

"Can I tell you a secret?" John leaned toward me as if he was about to whisper the secret in my ear.

Curious, I nodded.

He got very close to me and said softly, "Algebra is bullshit. It's just a waste of time."

I couldn't believe it. Jackson's dad really was cool! A huge grin crossed my face and I struggled not to laugh.

"I wouldn't worry about needing to learn it unless you plan to be an engineer, or else you'll never use it in real life. But you do want to keep your grades up, though, so if you need help, I can help you with some tutoring."

"Thanks, Mr. Pierce."

He frowned. "John, remember?"

"Oh, right. Sorry." I paused and forced a smile. "Thanks, John. That's very nice of you to offer, but I know you're busy."

"Don't be silly, Chloe. I'm not that busy," John assured me and I watched as he put his hand around my shoulder in a comforting gesture. The flesh of his palm was warm on my skin and for some reason, it made me a little nervous. Uncle Tom loved me, but he wasn't a big hugger like Aunt Betty was and he was rarely physically affectionate. I never knew my father. So feeling Jackson's father's arm around me made me wonder if this was what it was like to have a real dad and I allowed myself to lean into him.

"Chloe, you should know by now that nothing you could do would be an imposition to me. You've already given so much by being such a good friend to Jackson. You're a special person and I hope you know how much you mean to all of us."

"Thanks." I felt my cheeks flush, but inside my heart soared. They were the kinds of words that a girl just needed to hear from a male role model in her life, no matter how confident she was or how much self-esteem she had. I thought about Jackson and felt envious that he had a father.

Just then, as if he knew I was thinking about him, Jackson walked through the front door and set his football gear heavily on the floor of the entryway.

"Hey, Jackson. How was practice?" John cried out enthusiastically. He pulled his arm from around my shoulders rather abruptly in his rush to welcome Jackson home. But I hadn't really noticed. It made me smile to see the two of them have a chance to connect. I knew from personal experience how much it sucked to feel abandoned by your parents and it was rewarding to be able to witness this small moment between them.

"Fine," Jax said dully, then his face instantly brightened when our eyes met. " 'Sup, Clo? What are you doing here?"

What am I doing here? I knew there had been something I wanted to tell him, but at that moment, it'd slipped my mind.

Jackson's dad stepped in for me. "Chloe's struggling in math just a smidge and so I offered to give her some tutoring."

"Algebra?" Jackson asked and I nodded. "Who's your teacher?"

"Mr. Phillips," I responded.

Jackson gave a disgusted groan. "He's the worst! He talks a million words per minute and doesn't let anyone ask questions. I've got Beiderman; she's a lot better. They both use the same textbook and lesson plan. I can teach you everything you need to know, if you want. Come on, we can go over the stuff you're having problems with now."

I turned to Jackson's father and flashed him a grateful smile. "Thanks for the offer, Mr.—John, but looks like I don't need a tutor after all. I've got Jax!"

John's expression turned to one of disappointment, and I felt bad for taking his son's time away from him. *I'll make sure I don't stay too long so they can have some father and son time*, I thought to myself as I waved goodbye to Jackson's father.

As I followed Jackson to his room, I suddenly remembered why I had come over in the first place. Shoving the learner's permit in Jackson's face, I cried out happily, "Check out what I got today!"

"No way! Who'd you have to bribe to get that thing? Is it a fake?" Jackson ripped it from my hand and pretended to check it for authenticity, grinning all the while.

"No one, you jerk. I earned it myself and the lady at the DMV said I got one of the best scores she's seen all week. It's probably better than yours, so bite me!" I teased him back and we both laughed and fought with each other playfully in a battle over control of my learner's permit.

When we reached his room, Jackson handed it back to me and I saw his eyes were shining with pride. "I knew you'd ace it."

"No you didn't." I rolled my eyes. "You totally thought I was going to bomb. But I didn't." I couldn't resist throwing it in his face that he had been wrong with his prediction yesterday.

"No, I didn't. I just knew that telling you that would motivate you to study even harder. But I knew you'd pass the test and get your permit. You're one of the smartest girls I know."

"Yeah, well you're one of the biggest jerks I know!" I said, but he knew that was code for how much I really liked him. He really was the most amazing best friend anyone could ever ask for.

"Speaking of jerks, I'm sorry you got stuck here alone with my dad." Jackson made a face as he searched his room for his math textbook and a pencil.

"The coach made us all run extra laps today, so practice ran later than normal."

"Oh, it was fine. Your dad's really nice."

"You don't have to pretend with me." There was an edge to his voice I rarely heard.

"I'm not playing," I insisted. I don't know why, but I felt a strong need to defend his father. "You just don't see the situation clearly because you're too close to it."

"What situation is that?" Jax sounded annoyed.

"I know it sucks that your dad works such long hours and is never here for you and your mom, but did it ever occur to you that it sucks for him, too?"

"Whatever," he said dismissively, but I could tell from his voice that he didn't want to talk about his father anymore.

"It's obvious he misses you," I persisted, feeling a little envious of Jackson and a little annoyed that he took having a father for granted.

"How would you know? You don't even have annoying parents to know what's it's like!" he shot back.

His words shocked me and hit the mark right through my heart. I could tell he regretted them the moment they flew out of his mouth. His face went pale and his mouth was agape with the horror of his own cruelty.

My skin must have been equally pale and I could feel the hot tears brimming in my eyes. Somehow I was able to contain them just long enough to turn my back so he couldn't see them falling onto my cheeks.

"Clo, I'm so sorry! I didn't mean that." I heard the anguish in his voice and knew that he was truly filled with regret.

Good! He deserves to feel bad for saying something that awful. Not having parents of my own was something that I'd always been sensitive to. It was never the same when Aunt Betty and Uncle Tom came to parent-teacher conferences or Parent Nights. So to have my own best friend rub that in my face was almost too much to bear. I wanted to hate him for it.

But what happened next broke my resolve and made me instantly forgive him.

"Clo, I didn't mean it. Do you hear me? I didn't mean it! I'm so sorry. You have to forgive me. Say you forgive me." There was an unfamiliar tremor in Jackson's voice that moved me to turn around.

When I did, I saw that his face was red and twisted in remorse, and his eyes glistened with tears, something I'd almost never seen before. I could hardly believe that he was so upset at the thought of having hurt me that he was moved to tears. It was the first time I'd ever seen him like this and it touched my heart in a way nothing else could have.

"I forgive you, Jax," I said softly and he embraced me in a hug that was quick and hard.

"Really? You forgive me?" He sniffled, rubbing his face with my hair in a move that was gross yet tenderly sweet.

"Yeah, you're a jerk but there's nothing you could do that I couldn't forgive."

He hugged me harder. "Same goes for me. No matter what fights we may have or what mistakes we might make, I'll always forgive you and be your best friend," Jackson vowed.

I smiled and decided to change the subject to something lighter. "Now, are you going to help me with my algebra or not?"

Chapter Five

November 2001

Seventeen Years Old

Chloe

"Forget it. I change my mind! I don't wanna go to college. It's not worth the stress!" I cried out in despair. I felt buried alive under a mountain of forms. It turned out that filling out college entrance applications was a lot more complicated than I'd thought it would be and I was completely overwhelmed.

"If I can do it, you can do it." Jackson gave me a pat on the back that caused my pencil to slip on the form I was filling out.

"Test scores, essays, references, extra-curricular activities? Ugh. I don't have half of those things! And I haven't even started looking at scholarship applications." I huffed out a deep sigh as he sat down at the dining room table across from me and popped open a Mountain Dew.

"That doesn't mean you shouldn't try. What about all those dreams you had of traveling the world? Unless you're planning to join the army, I think you're going to want a college degree for that." Jackson flashed me one of his boyish grins. "And I think you'd be too much a distraction for the male soldier to be in the army," he taunted with a chuckle. Sometimes he had the most annoying way of being right about everything and it drove me crazy.

"Shut-up, smart-ass!" I tried to glare at him, but all I could do was smile. It made him laugh, and before I knew it, I was laughing too. He had the best way of lightening the mood when I got stressed out.

"Okay, now quit distracting me. I've got to get this application done if I want to get into Penn. You told me if I came over, you'd help."

"Actually, what I said was you should come over and we'll get my dad to help you. He's the one who works there, not me," Jackson corrected with that cocky grin of his.

"Did I hear someone talking about me?" Mr. Pierce suddenly strolled into the kitchen with a welcoming smile. "Hi, Chloe. Working on college applications, I see. How's that going?"

"Terrible!" I moaned. "I don't play any sports. I don't do any community service work. My grades are decent, but they're not amazing. Why would they ever accept me?"

"You're smart, caring, and a quick learner. You have a lot of great qualities any university would be a fool not to want. You just have to know how to put yourself in the best light," he explained. I blushed under the praise. It felt good to hear that. It gave me hope that maybe things weren't as impossible as I'd thought.

Jackson looked at his watch and said, "Hey, Dad, Sarah's coming over any minute. We have to work on our lines together for the play next month. Do you think you could help Chloe while I go study with Sarah?"

Ugh, I thought in annoyance. If I'd known that Sarah was coming over to hang out with Jackson, I probably wouldn't have stopped by. Sarah was Jackson's new girlfriend. They were recently cast as Romeo and Juliet in the school play, and after spending a lot of time together, she'd asked him out. She was blonde, with a perfect body, and she always wore her short cheerleader skirts around school. I didn't like her because I thought she had the most annoying personality. Still, she seemed to make Jackson happy, so I tried to keep my feelings of disgust hidden from him.

Mr. Pierce must have seen the roll of my eyes, because he put his hand on my shoulder and said kindly, "Sure, I'm always here to help."

Just then, Sarah showed up at the front door. She greeted Jackson with a kiss and pressed her body up against his. When she whispered something in his ear, Jackson abruptly said, "Okay, we're going up to my room to study. See ya later, Clo! Thanks again, Dad!"

He took Sarah by the hand and led her up to his bedroom, with her blonde ponytail bobbing behind her as she giggled. Her hips swayed suggestively as she walked, and when her giggles reached the end of the upstairs hallway where Jackson's room was, I heard the door shut behind them.

The whole scene made me want to gag. I thought about shouting out, *Practice safe sex!* just to embarrass Jackson. But with his father standing right there, I didn't think it was a good idea.

Mr. Pierce must have been thinking the same thing, because he shook his head and said, "I think I'm making a mistake letting those two be alone together. Tell me, do all girls your age act the way she does?"

"No, not all the girls," I said emphatically. "Don't let Sarah give you the wrong impression. There are plenty of girls at school that don't act like her, but guys do seem to pay more attention to popular girls like her."

"Ah, come on now, Chloe. A beautiful girl like you, with those eyes and that amazing smile? You must get asked out by every boy in school."

I felt myself blush under the compliment. I wasn't used to being noticed and complimented like that. It felt nice to be called beautiful, but a part of me wished that I could hear it more often from boys my own age, like Jackson. "Thanks, but I'm not like Sarah.

I'm too much of a klutz to be a cheerleader, and I'm pretty plain and not popular."

"I'm sure your boyfriend doesn't call you plain," he said with an encouraging smile.

I looked down, feeling bad for myself. "I don't have a boyfriend at the moment." There had been a few guys I'd gone on dates with, and had two guys that I'd called boyfriends in the past. But I was never that into them for things to get too serious.

"Well, believe me, you're far from plain. One day you'll be with a real man who will make you feel the way a woman should. You're incredible, Chloe—smart, funny, charming. One day, you'll have men lining up to be with you."

Something about the way he looked at me when he said all those things made me feel a little uneasy, and I felt my throat go dry. They were good compliments and I liked hearing them, but I was suddenly very aware of the fact that we were alone together.

"Well, I don't know how smart I am. I'm having a hard time with the essay for this application." I said as I took a small step back, and tried to change the subject back to the college applications. I cleared my throat. "If you have any pointers, I'd really appreciate if you could take a look."

He blinked, and as if he'd snapped out of a trance, he straightened up and gave a polite smile. "Yes." He cleared his throat. "Of course." Then he paused again, as if he were having a debate with himself about something. Seconds later, his expression changed again, and he flashed me a wider smile than before. "You know what?"

"What?" I frowned, confused by his behavior.

"You're my son's best friend. He practically treats you like his younger *sister*." He smiled.

I wasn't sure why, but I felt a ripple of disappointment wash over me when he mentioned the word, "sister." *Did Jax really think of me like his sister?* I forced myself to push aside the thought and turn my attention back to Mr. Pierce.

"...and as a prominent professor at Penn, I shouldn't just be giving you some advice. I should be doing more. A good recommendation letter from me can do more to bolster your application than anything else."

"You think so?" I looked at him hopefully, completely forgetting about the unease I'd felt moments ago.

"Definitely." He beamed confidently at me. "Chloe, I'll tell you what I can do for you. I'll write a recommendation for you that is so compelling, it will practically guarantee your acceptance at Penn."

"You'd do that for me?" I squealed with delight. "That's more than I could ask for. That would be so awesome if you can." My words rushed out quickly as I made no effort to hide my excitement. I felt like some of the worry that I'd felt for my future had just been lifted from my shoulders.

"Of course. It'd be my pleasure. Come on back into my office and I'll get you taken care of." His smile was warm and I eagerly followed him down the hall with the application in my hand.

His office was impressive, with a beautiful carved oak desk, shelves packed full of books, a leather sofa, and a state-of-the-art computer.

"You have a beautiful office."

He closed the door behind us and directed me to sit on the sofa by the window. I expected him to sit in his desk chair, but he surprised me by sitting on the cushion right next to me.

"So, I've known you since you were a child, but we haven't talked much in recent years," he started as he put a gentle hand on my knee and looked into my eyes. "What are you really passionate about? What are your goals and dreams?"

I didn't know how to answer his questions. They weren't the questions I'd expected him to ask. All I could think about was the feel of his firm, warm palm on my bare knee just below where my skirt ended, and it felt incredibly awkward. I knew he was just trying to help me, and I knew he was an affectionate person (he was more like Aunt Betty than he was like Uncle Tom in that respect), but I wasn't used to such an intimate gesture from an older man. I remembered Jackson once mentioned that his father was twenty when Jackson was born. Thirty-seven seemed so old.

Suddenly, I heard Jackson's voice shouting from down the hall, "Hey, Dad! Can Sarah stay for dinner?"

I wasn't sure why, but my stomach lurched when I saw the doorknob twist. A second later, the door swung open as Jackson looked in. Mr. Pierce got up from the couch and appeared to be brushing off some dust from his shirt. "Yeah, sure, Sarah can stay for dinner. Your friends are welcome here anytime."

For a split second, there was an odd expression on Jackson's face as he looked over at me and then at his father. But then it disappeared. "Great! You should stay too, Clo! We'll get a couple of large pizzas. My Dad can finish helping you with your application and then Sarah and I can act out the scene we've been practicing for you guys. It'll be like dinner and a show."

I stood up and fumbled for my papers. "Actually, I can't stay tonight. Sorry. I promised Aunt Betty I'd be home for dinner." I walked quickly to the door where Jackson stood. "In fact, I'd better get going now."

"What about your letter of recommendation?" Mr. Pierce asked.

As much as I needed the letter, at that moment, something inside me just wanted to get out of there. I wasn't sure why I felt that way, but I felt like I'd just done something wrong and was caught in the act.

"Thank you for the offer, but I didn't realize it was already so late. I guess I'll have to skip it."

"Don't be ridiculous. I'll still write it for you and you can pick it up tomorrow. You have everything going for you, Chloe. There's no reason you shouldn't get to go to Penn and make the most out of your life."

"Thanks." I flushed. I suddenly felt bad for feeling awkward around Mr. Pierce. He wasn't a bad man. Maybe I was just upset about Jackson getting it on with Sarah upstairs and it put the thoughts of sex on my mind. What I thought had just happened between me and Mr. Pierce was nothing more than my own imagination. Still, the idea of coming back to get the letter from him made me a little uneasy. *If only there was a way to make sure Jackson would be here, too.*

"Sounds great. What time will you be home from football tomorrow, Jax? Maybe we can hang out when I stop by." I looked at Jackson expectantly, hoping I sounded casual.

"Sorry, Clo." He shrugged. "Can't. We've got late practice every night until the playoffs. If you want, I can just bring the letter with me to school tomorrow and give it to you that way?"

"Perfect!" I sighed with relief.

***

The next day in homeroom, when Jackson handed me Mr. Pierce's letter of recommendation, I felt like the worst person in the world for not wanting to personally get it from him in person. Every line of the letter of recommendation made me sound like a far better person than I knew I was. It was very generous and kind of him to have spent the time to write this recommendation and I knew I should really show more appreciation and gratitude for all his help.

As I tucked the letter of recommendation neatly between the pages of my biology textbook, I made a promise to myself: *If I get accepted into Penn, I'll really need to properly thank Mr. Pierce for help. I'll owe him big time.*

Chapter Six

June 2003

Eighteen Years Old

Chloe

I waved Jackson down as I saw him searching the crowd for me outside of the high school auditorium. When our eyes met, his face lit up and he immediately walked over to where I stood with Aunt Betty, Uncle Tom, and my cousin, Charlie.

"That was a great graduation speech, Jackson." Uncle Tom patted Jackson on the back when he came over.

"Harvard's going to be lucky to have you going to school there," Aunt Betty chimed in as she pulled Jackson in for a warm hug.

Jackson smiled, beaming with pride. "Thanks. I'm excited to finally graduate high school and start college."

He then glanced over at me with his familiar boyish grin and winked. "Congrats, Clo."

"Congrats, Jax." I smiled back. "Uncle Tom's right. That was a great speech, Mr. Valedictorian. You made me cry."

"But you cry about everything," he teased.

I punched him in the arm, harder than normal this time. "I do not. Ass."

He laughed. "I'm going to miss your daily physical abuse when I'm at Harvard and you're at Penn."

"Me too." We shared a meaningful gaze and I wondered if we'd always be best friends like this.

"Congratulations, man." My cousin Charlie shook Jackson's hand. Charlie then smiled over at me. "Who knew Chloe would have a genius for a best friend?"

I laughed. "I'm pretty sure I should take that as an insult, Charlie." I made a face at him.

"Hey, you know I'm just teasing." Charlie laughed sheepishly and pulled me into his arms for a bear hug. "You got into Penn, kiddo. That's a pretty good indication that you're pretty much a genius yourself. You know I'm super proud of you."

I giggled as I pulled away from him. "It's so good to see you, Charlie. Thanks for coming to my graduation. It means so much to me."

Charlie was Aunt Betty and Uncle Tom's son. He had just turned twenty-nine recently and had been working as an attorney at a prestigious law firm in Chicago for about a year now. Before that, he went to UCLA in California for law school for three years. But even though he had a busy life, he'd always made time to fly back home to visit his parents and to see me. I always loved it when he visited. Not only was he funny and easy to talk to, I loved having him around the house. The love he shared with Aunt Betty and Uncle Tom was how I'd always pictured the perfect family to be. So it always made me smile when I got the chance to see them interact together as a family unit.

We all laughed and talked excitedly for several minutes about the graduation ceremony and our plans for college. Then Aunt Betty and Uncle Tom went to go talk to some of the teachers and Charlie went to the restroom. Jackson used this opportunity to pull me aside to talk.

"Clo, I have something for you. Are you free in an hour?"

"What is it?"

"Just a little something I think you'll like," he answered vaguely.

I looked at him suspiciously. "I thought we'd agreed not to do gift exchanges for graduation?"

He snickered. "Who said anything about it being a graduation gift?"

I rolled my eyes. "What is it?"

"It's a surprise. Meet me out at our spot in an hour?"

I faked an annoyed look. "Fine. I guess you do always seem to get what you want," I teased.

He chuckled. "Sometimes." Then he paused briefly. "But not everything." He looked at me in a way that made my heart pound faster against my chest, and I wondered why he had this effect on me.

Before I could ask him what he'd meant by his last comment or work through what I was feeling, someone came around from behind Jackson and interrupted us.

"Great speech, Mr. Hotshot. Can you sign my graduation program so I can have it before you become famous?" Amber joked as she excitedly swung her arm around Jackson's shoulder.

The moment I saw Amber, I felt my happy mood disappear.

"Thanks, Amber." Jackson flashed her a smile but took a deliberate step away from her.

I saw a flicker in Amber's eyes as she smiled over at Jackson, and I knew that I wasn't the only one who had noticed Jackson's subtle movement. While forcing myself to keep a straight face, I felt a small surge of triumph flow through me, and at that moment, I had an intense urge to throw my arms around Jackson and give him a big hug.

Even though, personally, Jackson thought I was overreacting and holding a childhood grudge, he knew I didn't like Amber and stood by my side. I knew deep down that I'd been holding a grudge against Amber, but I also knew that sometimes the embarrassment and hurt a person experienced when they were younger could leave permanent marks and would never truly go away. That was how I felt about Amber. She was the girl who had made fun of the cigarette burns my mom had accidentally made on my overalls on my first day of school in first grade after I'd moved in with Aunt Betty and Uncle Tom. She had then pretended to be nice to me and invited me to eat lunch with her and her friends, but then had called me dirty and made fun of my clothes. She was the girl who had gotten the entire cafeteria to laugh at me that day. And ever since that very first day we'd met, she'd never been nice to me. Sometimes she'd pretend to be, like when Jackson was around, but I knew she was faking it. I think she'd always blamed me for the way Jackson had treated her that day in front of the entire school when he'd come to my rescue after I fell on the cafeteria floor.

"Hi, Chloe." Amber flashed me a bright smile, showing off her perfect pearly whites.

I snapped out of my thoughts in time to force myself to return a polite smile. "Hey, Amber."

"Congrats on graduating. I never thought we'd all make it to this day, did you?" she asked with a giggle. There was a smirk on her face as she eyed me up and down.

I felt my blood start to boil at what I knew she was trying to imply with her words. Since we were in first grade, she had always thought she was better than me and was never shy about voicing that opinion to me in her subtle, condescending way.

I wanted to respond and put her in her place, but Jackson stopped me and spoke up first. "Congrats on also getting into Harvard, Amber. I had no idea you had applied or that they accepted applications after the first of January." I could tell from the tone in his voice that he was mocking her.

"They don't, actually. I missed the deadline by a few months. But it was the least Harvard could do, seeing as my dad's an alumnus and was one of their top financial donors last year." Amber shrugged like it wasn't a big deal.

I smiled to myself just then. I knew immediately why Jackson had made his comment. In his own way, he had been defending me against Amber's comments by forcing Amber to admit to her own failures. But his attempt was lost on Amber as she seemed to freely and unabashedly admit to not getting into Harvard on her merits alone.

Then she turned to me and frowned. "Too bad you can't also join us at Harvard, Chloe. That would have been so much fun!"

The sheer lack of sincerity in her voice grated against my patience. But before I could say anything, Jackson stopped me again.

"Hey, Clo. There're my parents waving us down. Let's go say hi." He grabbed my hand in a rush and pulled me away from Amber. "See ya later, Amber," he said quickly with a wave.

"See you at Harvard, Jackson," she called after us in a singsong voice. Even with my back turned to her as Jackson ushered me away, I could picture the smug smirk across Amber's face as she watched us leave.

"Why did you keep interrupting me, Jax?" I felt annoyed that I didn't get a chance to vent my anger out on that bitch.

"Clo, I could tell you were getting upset, and really, it's not worth it."

"It sure feels worth it to me," I retorted in disagreement as I imagined how much better I'd feel if I'd said something mean to Amber. Maybe if she came back with more of her bitchiness, I would have even punched her in the face.

"Come on, Clo. It's our graduation. It's not worth causing a scene in front of everyone or wasting your time on her. We're both about to move away for college. Let's make the best of our free time before we start school."

I huffed out a sigh of frustration. I always hated when Jackson was right, especially when I wanted so badly for him to be wrong.

"Besides," he continued, "Amber's harmless. I know she rubs you the wrong way. She definitely has a strong personality. But really she's not all that bad. I think you two just got off on the wrong foot from the very beginning. She's not as bad as she used to be."

I rolled my eyes, annoyed that Jackson was defending the closest thing I had to a nemesis. "Jax, how can you say that? She's just as bad if not worse than she was when we were in first grade. She's just more subtle about it and she acts different when you're around. But she's always giving me her condescending bitchy look."

Jackson swung his arm around my shoulder and chuckled. "Are you sure it's not just her Resting Bitch Face?"

I couldn't help but laugh at his question. "Yes, I'm sure, unless there's a Resting Bitch Face Only When Chloe's Around," I joked back.

He laughed, even though we both knew how bad my attempt of a joke was. "Come on, looks like people are starting to leave. Come over and say hi to my parents before you head home."

"Sure." I smiled over at him, feeling happy that his arm was still around my shoulder as we walked over to his parents.

"Congratulations, son." Mr. Pierce patted Jackson on the back and they exchanged an enthusiastic handshake.

"We're so proud of you, Jackson!" Mrs. Pierce gave Jackson a hug and kiss. Then she turned to me with a bright smile. "Congratulations to you too, Chloe!

It's a wonderful accomplishment," Mrs. Pierce exclaimed as she gave me a quick hug.

"Thanks, Mrs. Pierce." I flashed her a wide smile. "That means a lot coming from you." Mrs. Pierce worked so many hours as a partner at her law firm that I'd never really seen too much of her. I was glad that she made time to be here to see Jackson graduate and give his valedictorian speech. I knew Jackson would have been disappointed if she hadn't made it.

"Definitely a great accomplishment you should be proud of, Chloe," Mr. Pierce said as he put his hand on my shoulder and squeezed it. "Penn is lucky to have you."

I gave a friendly smile as I took a step back. "Thanks, Mr. Pierce. I really appreciate all your help with my college application to Penn." No matter how many times Jackson's father insisted that I call him by his first name, I always felt more comfortable addressing him as Mr. Pierce. It was what felt more natural to me. So when I heard myself call him by Mr.

Pierce, I waited for his inevitable "Call me John" correction.

But to my surprise, he didn't correct me this time.

"Kim and I are always more than happy to help Jackson's friends whenever we can." I watched him slip his hand around Mrs. Pierce's waist and kissed her gently on the cheeks.

"Thank you. That's so nice of you guys." I smiled at them politely.

"College can be a bit daunting sometimes, Chloe. Don't forget I'm a professor at Penn. So if you ever need any help or advice on anything, or you just need someone to talk to, my door is always open for you, okay?"

"Sure. Thanks, Mr. Pierce. That's too generous of you." I smiled at him with gratitude. I didn't know why, but something told me that this was an offer I wouldn't take him up on.

***

About an hour later, I met Jackson at "our spot"—the park with the small lake that was close to our houses.

I found him sitting on the lush, green grass looking out onto the lake when I arrived.

I quietly tiptoed over to him and covered his eyes with my hands from behind.

"Guess who?"

"Mmm, this is hard. I don't seem to recognize this voice at all," he responded thoughtfully.

I didn't need to see the boyish grin on his face to know he was teasing.

"Ass," I teased.

"Fine. Fine. Fine. You win." He threw his hands up in the air like he was finally giving in after some pressure. "It's Pippi Longstocking, isn't it?" He grabbed my hands with his and pulled them off his eyes before spinning around to face me.

When he saw the pout on my face, he started to laugh uncontrollably.

"Yes!" he whooped in excitement. "I guessed right!"

"Har, har, har. Very funny." I rolled my eyes. "I look nothing like Pippi Longstocking."

"Really?" He sounded like he wasn't convinced as he cocked his head and studied me. "Hmm. Okay, maybe you're right. You are a little cuter than Pippi." He paused. "Plus, your hair's not braided in pigtails at the moment."

I scoffed at his comment, but I felt my heart skip a beat when he said I was cuter.

"So why did you ask me to meet you here?" I asked, changing the subject.

"Come on, let's walk around the park. It's so nice out today. I'm really going to miss coming here with you."

When he got up from the grass, he bent his arm to the side and offered it to me. I smiled and curled my arm around his, letting him lead us through the grass toward the paved pathway that went along the lake.

I looked around the park and drew in a deep breath of air through my nose and shut my eyes. "You're right, Jax. I'm really going to miss it here."

"Me too."

The mood between us seemed to turn melancholy as we walked down the path arm-in-arm, taking in the familiar surroundings in silence.

"You know what I'll really miss?" Jackson asked, breaking the sober stillness. I could tell by the tone in his voice that he wanted to brighten things up.

"What?" I looked over at him expectantly.

He grinned. "I'm really going to miss Aunt Betty."

"Oh." I frowned, not expecting him to say that. "Who else are you going to miss?" I asked with a smile, playfully fishing for the answer I wanted to hear.

I watched his face twist as he thought about it. "Hmm. I can't think of anyone else, actually."

"Jerk." I glared at him and slapped him across his hard chest with my free hand.

"What?" He gave me an innocent look of confusion. "It's true. I feel like I've been spoiled by her cooking. I'm really going to miss her." He paused to let out an exaggerated sigh. "You know? She's the added perk in being your friend." He stifled a chuckle as he looked away briefly. I could tell that he was only half-joking.

I snorted and tried to respond in a serious tone. "Well, I must have gotten the short end of the stick then, because there's no added perk in being your friend."

"Ouch!" Jackson gripped his chest like he was in physical pain. But within seconds, he exploded in laughter, causing me to lose my own composure and I joined him in a fit of laughter.

After several minutes, we finally calmed down from the outburst. Then I remembered something I'd wanted to try. I turned to Jackson without saying a word.

I could tell he was confused by my actions but he didn't question me at first.

I looked into his eyes and held his gaze in silence. For some reason, I suddenly felt my skin prickle with nerves, which wasn't something I'd expected or planned for.

He studied me, his lips curled into boyish grin. "What?" His eyes darted to his left and then to his right before returning back to my gaze. I could tell he was a little nervous.

"Nothing," I whispered and flashed him a coy smile. I held back the urge to laugh. He looked so cute right then, squirming and feeling uneasy.

"Okay...." He paused and frowned. "T—then why are you staring me like that?"

Finally, I couldn't take it anymore and I started to giggle. "You know you can be so adorable when you get nervous."

He narrowed his eyes at me. "You're an ass, you know that?" he teased. "Pippi Longstocking."

"Hey!" I punched him playfully on the chest. "You know I don't like to be called that. Be nice!"

He laughed. "Only if you will."

I rolled my eyes. "Okay. Okay. Okay. You're so sensitive." I huffed sarcastically.

"So why were you staring at me without blinking?"

I giggled. "Fine, I'll tell you. So I read this science article this morning—"

"Nerd," he cut me off with a snicker before I could finish.

"Takes one to know one," I shot back. "Hater."

"I just speak the truth." His boyish grin returned on his face. "Nerd."

I pushed him playfully. "For your information, you're not automatically a nerd if you read." Jackson loved to tease me for how much I enjoyed reading.

"That's what nerds like you say to try to convince people they're not one." He chuckled.

"You're annoying." I began to pout, feeling a little agitated by his persistent teasing.

As if sensing my growing impatience, his expression softened. "Come on, don't be like that. You know I was just teasing."

I folded my arms across my chest. "Well, sometimes you go too far and it can get annoying."

"You're right. Sometimes I get carried away in the back and forth teasing that I don't know when to stop." He shrugged innocently. "I'm sorry."

It was hard to be upset with Jax for too long. I knew he had a good heart and never meant to make me upset. "It's all right."

"So what did you read in the science article?"

"Oh, right." For a moment there, I had forgotten all about the article. "Well the article said that people who love each other can sync up their heart rates by staring into each other's eyes. I thought that was pretty cool and wanted to try it." When I heard my explanation out loud, I realized how stupid it must have sounded.

"Oh." Jackson looked taken aback by my comments. There was an expression on his face that I couldn't read, and I immediately felt a wave of panic prickle down my spine.

"Yeah," I hastily added, "so I wanted to see if it'd work for people who didn't love each other." I wasn't sure why I blurted out my last comment, but somehow, I couldn't help myself.

"Right." That was all he said in response before we fell into another period of silence as we continued to walk along the path.

As I began to get lost in my own thoughts, I was hit with a powerful sense of nostalgia.

"Jax?" My voice was close to a whisper.

He turned his head to look at me. "Yeah?"

"Promise me we'll stay in touch." I turned to meet his warm gaze.

"Don't be silly, Clo. Of course we'll stay in touch."

"Just promise me," I insisted.

He smiled. "Okay. I promise you that not only will we stay in touch, but we'll stay best friends. Don't be a worry-wart, Clo. Why would you even think that we wouldn't?" I could detect a hint of concern in his voice.

I looked away, pretending I had some dust in my eyes as I wiped away the tears that had collected there.

It took me a few moments before I was able to respond without fear of losing it in front of him. "It's just that the people who are the most important to me—or should be the most important to me—either were never in my life, or they end up leaving me behind and never returning." I was thinking of my dad and mom.

"Come on, Clo. You know I won't leave you behind."

"Yeah." I looked away again, trying to work through my feelings. I knew I was being melodramatic and silly, and maybe a tad morbid, but it felt like an end of an era for Jackson and me. I was worried that when we both actually left for college, things would change—*we* would change—and everything about our friendship would just be memories, intangible parts of ourselves, figments of our past that we might be able to recall, but could never return back to.

"Don't think like that, Clo." Jackson squeezed my hand as he slowed to a stop. He smiled down at me when our eyes met.

"Why did we stop here?" I asked as I looked around. We had walked up one of the small metal bridges that arched across a narrow section of the lake.

Instead of answering me, he grinned and followed my question with a question of his own.

"Do you remember the first day you were nice to me?"

"You mean the first day you were nice *to me*?" I corrected him, knowing he was referring to my first day of school during first grade.

"Let's agree to disagree on that point." He laughed. "Well, that was the first day you took my hand when I helped you up from the cafeteria floor."

"So?" I wasn't sure where he was going with his question.

"Well, when you took my hand, it meant you trusted me, and I somehow knew that from that day forward we'd be best friends."

I raised an eyebrow and looked at him dubiously. "You knew all that from just me taking your hand?"

"Well, the way I see it, the moment you decided to take my hand was the moment I knew you trusted me." He then paused and gazed into my eyes. "I know you're worried about the future, Clo. I am, too. So I'm asking you now to close your eyes and take my hand again."

I looked at him suspiciously, unsure what he had planned.

"Come on, Clo. Show me you trust me. Close your eyes and take my hand."

"Okay, Jax, but no funny business. Don't you dare push me in the lake," I warned before I closed my eyes.

He chuckled. "That wasn't what I was thinking...*but* thanks for putting that thought in my head." The playfulness in his voice eased my nerves as

I kept my eyes closed and reached my hands out in front of me.

I felt his warm hands touch mine and an intense sensation rushed through me. Before I could figure out what the feeling meant, Jackson turned my hands around and positioned my opened palms together so that my hands formed a bowl shape. Seconds later I felt him place a cool, metal object in between my hands.

"This is the surprise I had for you." From the sound of his low, hushed voice, I could sense how surprisingly close he was to me.

"This is what you got for me?" I asked in confusion. It feels like a lock—maybe a padlock, but why would he be getting me a lock?

"Open your eyes."

I opened my eyes and saw him looking at me with a twinkle of eager excitement in his eyes. I forced myself to pull my gaze from his warm emerald eyes and looked down at the object in my palms.

To my surprise, I was right. It was a padlock.

But it wasn't like the padlock I'd used for my locker in school. This lock was painted red and was in the shape of a heart.

"What is it?" I looked back at Jackson expectantly.

He beamed at me. "It's a love lock."

"A love lock?" My stomach flipped when I heard his words.

"Do you remember that pact we made when we were thirteen?"

My eyes grew wide. I was too surprised to respond verbally, so I just nodded.

Of course I remembered the night we made the pact. I remembered it perfectly like it'd happened just yesterday. I could still see the glow of the soft, colorful lights that moved across my bedroom ceiling that Jackson had created to mimic the Northern Lights. I remembered the things he'd said to me, the promises he'd made me, and the unforgettable kiss we'd shared. But for some reason, after that night, we'd never talked about the pact again—or that kiss we'd shared. After a while, I'd convinced myself that Jackson had forgotten about the pact and the kiss—or worse, he had regretted it and wanted me to forget about them.

So to hear him bring up the pact we'd made that night five years ago paralyzed me with shock.

"Well," he continued, "I know you've been nervous about going to different colleges and how that'd affect our friendship. I know you're scared about being alone. I just want to let you know that I have those same feelings. And that is why I had this made for you—for us. I wanted to remind you of our pact and my promise to you. Even though we haven't talked about it since we first agreed to it five years ago, I meant every word I said. If we're both single by the time we're thirty, I promise to marry you."

Tears welled up in my eyes as I looked into his eyes. "Oh, Jax. I meant it, too," I whispered. "You're my best friend, and I can't imagine being happier than when I'm with you."

"I feel the same way. So I heard about this tradition with love locks recently where two people will lock a padlock against the railing of a bridge or gate and then throw away the keys. It's supposed to symbolize unbreakable love." He moved closer to me, leaving only a few inches between us. "I got this love lock for us because I wanted to let you know that I'll always be here for you, and you don't ever need to worry about being lonely."

He reached for the red heart-shaped lock in my hands and turned it over. "I had it inscribed for us. Take a look."

Completely blown away by his touching gesture, I was speechless as I looked down at the lock and saw the inscription etched on the back:

Jax & Clo

June 2003

Unbreakable Friendship & Love.

Promise to Marry in 2014.

"Jax, this is the sweetest thing anyone's ever given me." Tears blinded me as I threw my arms around him, burying my face into his neck and inhaling his inviting scent.

"Clo," he whispered in my ear. "I'm so happy that you like it."

I pulled away to look up at him and smiled. "Like it? Jax, I *love* it. I've been so worried about how things will change with our friendship when college starts. This is exactly the type of reassurance I needed."

He beamed at me. "So does that mean you still agree to the pact?" He looked at me hopefully.

I giggled, surprised that he'd even think that I could possibly say no. "Of course, silly." I looked down at the love lock. "So what exactly are we supposed to do?"

He took the lock from me and we walked up to the edge of the bridge where the railing was. Then he held my hands with his and looked into my eyes.

"Clo, you've been my best friend for the past eleven years, and I know you'll be my best friend for the rest of my life. I don't know where life will take us, but I know that we will always be by each other's sides. We made a pact when we were thirteen to marry each other if we are both single when we turn thirty. Today, we're going to seal that pact with this love lock, which will symbolize our unbreakable friendship, love, and promise to marry each other."

He handed me the love lock. "Do you want to do the honors?"

I nodded and took the lock and latched it against the railing.

"Promise?" I looked into his rich, emerald eyes—those eyes that always had a way of making me feel at home.

"Promise." He beamed at me and placed his hands on top of mine as we both secured the love lock onto the bridge railing and locked it in place.

I removed the key from the lock. We both looked at the tiny key and then at each other and smiled. He gave me a nod before I threw the key over the railing and watched it disappeared into the lake without a sound.

"Looks like you'll be stuck with me if we're both single in twelve years," I joked.

Instead of laughing along, he surprised me as he pulled me into his arms and whispered in my ear, "You're my best friend, Clo. You won't ever have to worry about being alone. I'll always be here for you when you need me."

He pulled back a little so he could face me, leaving only a few inches between us as we gazed into each other's eyes. As his hand gently pushed a loose strand of hair behind my ear, I felt an exquisite tingle run down my body from where his fingers grazed my skin. He kissed me sweetly on my forehead, causing my body to buzz with emotions. As his face lingered near mine, I thought he was about to kiss me.

He didn't.

I knew I should feel relieved that he didn't kiss me, we were just friends and I didn't think he liked me like that, but I couldn't help feeling a tinge disappointment wash through me when he didn't.

But as he pulled me deep into his arms, and I sank into his inviting embrace, those feelings of disappointment was overshadowed by the happiness that spread through me like a warm blanket on a cold day. Despite everything that'd happened in my life, I felt hopeful. I knew that no matter what the future held for me, Jackson would always be there.

"Here's to your thirtieth birthday," he said playfully when he finally pulled away.

"And yours, too," I added.

"Well, not exactly." He paused and grinned—that same boyish grin from the first day we met, the same boyish grin I'd come to know so well in the past eleven years, the same boyish grin that made my heart soar with happiness.

"What do you mean?" I feigned a frown, knowing too well he was being a smart-ass.

"Well, seeing as I'm eight months older than you, our pact won't start when *I* turn thirty." He chuckled smugly. "So I'm rooting for your thirtieth."

I laughed and slapped him gently against his chest.

As we slowly walked back to the paved pathway and followed it back along the lake, the warm crimson sun began to disappear over the horizon. But instead of feeling the cool night's air against my skin, the delirious warmth of happiness seemed to spread through my entire body, and I felt more alive and happy than I could ever imagine possible.

Chapter Seven

September 2003

Nineteen Years Old

Jackson

"You did not tell her that!" She laughed hysterically on the other end of the line.

"I was just telling it like it is." I snickered as I stretched out on top of my bed. It felt nice to hear Chloe's laughter.

"So you guys didn't have sex, then?" There was a hesitation in her question that I found troubling.

"Hell no!" I scrunched my face in disgust, and then felt a wave of disappointment when I realized that she couldn't actually see my reaction.

"But I thought all the guys in your dorm think Megan's a ten?"

"She may be hot, but you've met her. She's pretty wild and loves the attention. I'm pretty sure in the past four weeks since classes started, she's slept with half the single guys on the floor and probably countless other guys on the other floors in just this residence hall."

Chloe had met Megan—a girl in my freshman class who lived on my dorm floor—when Chloe came to visit me four weeks ago. Her fall semester classes had started a week before mine and on her first weekend, she'd taken the train up to visit me during Harvard's Welcome Week before our classes officially started. During her visit, we'd bumped into Megan at one of the infamous Welcome Week frat parties. Megan had come up to us to say hi because she said she'd seen me earlier that morning in our dorm. I knew pretty quickly that Chloe didn't like Megan, and even though I didn't want to admit to it, I wanted to think that the reason was because Chloe was jealous and threatened by Megan. Of course, she had no reason to feel jealous or threatened—Megan couldn't hold a candle to Chloe when it came to anything that mattered to me. But still, it was nice to imagine Chloe wanting me more because another girl was showing me interest. So even though I didn't care for Megan, I secretly enjoyed mentioning girls like Megan to Chloe because I wanted to see how Chloe would react. liked to see Chloe's reactions. talking about other girls with Chloe because I enjoyed her reactions.

"But what if you hurt her feelings when you rejected her like that?"

I could hear the mixture of curiosity and amusement in Chloe's voice.

"Well, I think she had it coming," I said frankly. "If she's going to ask me point blank if I want to take her back to my dorm room for a night I won't forget when we've previously only talked briefly maybe three or four times, of course I'm going to tell her she's right, I won't forget it because three of the guys on my floor have already told me their nights with her in detail."

"Jax, you can be such an ass sometimes!"

I chuckled. "Touché. I've never denied that."

"So have you met any other girls at Harvard?" she asked. The interest and curiosity in her voice made me smile.

"Nah. I'm not really interested in any of these girls."

"Really? So are you interested in guys, then?" she teased.

I laughed. I knew she didn't really think that. "Hell no! I'm a women-only type of guy."

She giggled. "How can you say that if you're not interested in any?"

"I never said I'm not interested in *any*," I corrected her. "I'm just not interested in any of these girls here at Harvard." I smiled as I closed my eyes and tried to picture Chloe's face.

"So who are you interested in, then?" she asked.

"That's my secret to keep," I teased. "But if you must know, you do know her, and she's incredible."

I heard her giggle, knowing I was referring to her. But I wondered if she thought I was just humoring her. Since we sealed our promise to marry each other with the love lock a few months ago, we'd been teasing each other about our pact, and our running joke between us was where we'd tease one another on who would break this promise by dating and marrying someone else, and who would make this a promise to keep.

As if to agree with my suspicions, she teased, "Don't tell me you're holding out for me so you can keep our promise?"

"Nah," I casually said. Even though I let out a laugh, I felt a little deflated by her question. I knew it's something we teased each other about. But it had become a constant reminder that she didn't really know how I felt about her.

"That's good," she said a little too quickly. "I don't want you to feel obligated to keep your promise and tell me you're not interested in someone." The tone in her voice was playful and teasing.

"You mean because of our pact?"

"Yeah."

Trying to adopt her playfulness, I teased her back. "Nah. The only reason I made that pact was because I want to use my thirtieth birthday as a warning of my old age. It'll be like an alarm to let me know I have eight months to find a wife before I have to be stuck with you for the rest of my life." I forced out a chuckle.

"You're so mean," she whined.

For a split second, I wondered if this wasn't what she wanted to hear. "Oh, you know I don't mean it," I quickly added just in case. "You know I'd be lucky to end up with someone as cool as you."

She laughed. "You're such a kiss-up. I don't believe a word that comes out of your mouth."

I laughed along, but on the inside, I wished she didn't think that way. I wished she knew the truth.

I had wanted to tell Chloe that I wanted to be more than just friends several months earlier when we'd sealed our childhood promise to marry each other with the love lock. But at the last minute, I'd chickened out because I started to wonder if the timing was right. I knew living six hours away from one another was already going to be a difficult adjustment for us as best friends. I wasn't sure if tacking on a possible relationship—assuming she'd even be interested—during such a transitional and unstable period in our lives would be too much for us to handle. Plus, I wasn't completely sure how she'd felt about me—whether she loved me the way I loved her or just as a best friend. So I knew telling her how I really felt and what I really wanted would be a risk, and it was something I only had one shot at. Because once I confessed my feelings, I could never take the words back, and if she didn't feel the same way, it could forever change the dynamic of our friendship.

"Anyway, all jokes aside, are you okay, Jax?" Chloe's voice changed to something more serious.

I knew what she wanted to talk about and I really didn't want to talk about it. "Yes. I'm fine."

She paused. "Well, you know that if you need to talk about it, I'm here for you."

"There's really nothing to talk about, Clo. Classes have been great. College has been great. You know I've been busy going to a lot of the rush events for the fraternities. I really like one of the houses, and I hope I get a bid from them. Things couldn't be better."

There was another pause on her end. "Jax…your parents just told you they're getting a divorce a month ago. I know you had your issues with your dad, but I know you didn't want to see your parents' marriage end. I know you're in a lot of pain but you don't want to admit to it because you think it's a show of weakness, but it's not, Jax. It's—"

"Stop!" My voice came out louder than I intended. "I really don't want to talk about it."

"Okay, Jax…I'm here if you need me."

I felt a little annoyed and I knew she was probably still thinking about it. She probably wished I were one of those sappy guys who was more open with their feelings and talked about all the pain and sadness they felt. But I wasn't one of those guys. I didn't want to admit to her that I was blindsided by my parents' divorce. I knew things weren't perfect between them, but I'd never imagined they'd get a divorce. I'd never imagined they'd stop loving each other. They'd broken the news about a few weeks before I left for Harvard. My dad had already found a place of his own in the city, closer to the university. He'd moved out a week later. I knew Chloe had been worried about me. She'd call me a lot to check in on me. She'd been trying to get me to talk about it. She'd even come to visit me the weekend after her first week of classes. She had tried to play it off—that it'd been her intention to visit me that weekend all along—but I knew she had wanted to check out some clubs and activities at her campus that first weekend, and she'd missed a lot of the club sign-ups and informational meetings that happened that weekend in order to visit me instead. I knew she was doing all this because she cared. But I just didn't want to talk about it. The divorce was just too fresh in my mind. It was something I had no control or say over. It was what it was, and there was nothing I could do about it. Talking about it wouldn't change anything. Talking about it would only remind me that it happened, and I didn't want to think about it.

"Thanks, Clo. You don't have to worry. It is what it is. I'm over it."

"Are you sure?"

"Yes," I said flatly, annoyed by her persistence. "Oh yeah, guess what?" I knew just then exactly what I could say to take her mind off my parents' divorce.

"What?"

"Amber says hi."

"Amber?" I could tell she became more alert at the mention of her name.

"Yeah. It turns out that we have English Lit together."

"Oh. How come you didn't mention this before?"

There was an accusatory tone in her voice that I didn't like, and I was immediately on the defensive.

"She never came up in conversation and I forgot. What's your deal with her, anyway?" I grimaced when I heard my question come out.

"Nothing," she shot back quickly. "I just think she's a bitch."

I let out a sigh. "I'm sorry, Clo. I know. That came out wrong. I know you don't like her, but I think she's really matured since high school."

"Yeah, maybe," she said half-heartedly.

Then I let out an uncontrollable yawn. I looked over at the clock on the wall and realized it was one in the morning. We'd been on the phone for over two hours now.

"Hey, I think I'm about to crash, Clo." I yawned again. "I have an eight o'clock class in the morning."

"Yeah, me too," I admitted, catching myself yawn as well. "I'm pretty tired."

"Call you later this week?" I suggested.

"Okay. Sure. Oh and don't forget to think about November."

I smiled. "Clo, I've already told you. There's nothing to think about. It's a done deal."

"Jax, just double check with your classes. I know there are a lot of midterms and papers due in November. I wouldn't want your grades to suffer just so you can visit me then."

I shook my head and laughed. "Clo, don't be ridiculous. Of course I'm going to visit you that weekend. It's your birthday. We've never celebrated a birthday apart since we've known each other. I wouldn't miss it for the world."

"Okay." I could hear the happiness and excitement in her voice. "You promise?"

"Yes," I laughed. "I promise."

Chapter Eight

November 2003

Eighteen Years Old

Chloe

First semester at Penn was hard for me—harder than I'd thought it would be.

I made a few friends at my dorm, but not many and no one I felt I'd really bonded with. All my freshman year classes at Penn were so large, with well over two hundred students in each lecture, that it was impossible to make friends with anyone in class. I should know, I'd tried to make conversation with a few girls I'd seen in class, and they had all smiled and responded back politely, but made no efforts to prolong the conversation before rushing out of the lecture hall. Many of the other freshmen on my floor in my residence hall seemed to be meeting new people through the Greek system—if they were pledging a fraternity or sorority— or through a club or social group they'd joined during the first week of classes. There had been a few clubs that I had wanted to check out, but I ended up missing their scheduled informational meetings and sign-ups because I had gone to visit Jackson instead. I tried to go to one of the club's second events two weeks later, but it seemed like people had already made friends with each other from the first introduction meeting and had met up to hang out a few times between the first and second club event. I'd ended up leaving the event feeling like an outsider, and it brought up the same feelings of insecurity and loneliness that I'd felt during my first day at my new school when I'd moved in with Aunt Betty and Uncle Tom. It wasn't the type of feeling I wanted to feel, and I never ended up checking out the other clubs I had also been interested in.

And after a while, it felt harder and harder to make friends with people because as people started to form their social circles and routines, they became less willing to make time and space for new friends.

What made the first few months of college even worse was Jackson. I really missed him. He had started pledging a fraternity a few weeks into the start of the semester and with every passing week, I'd hear less and less often from him. And when I did hear from him, it was usually just a quick text or email, and rarely a call. The few times I'd actually heard his voice, I could barely get a few words in before he said he had to go.

But I didn't fault him for being busy. College was supposed to be busy and fun. Even though my first semester wasn't panning out the way I'd wanted or imagined, it wasn't fair to blame Jackson for it, or expect him to not enjoy his own college experience. I never told him that I hadn't made many friends yet, and I wasn't sure if I would, even if he was around more to talk to. I didn't want him to feel bad or guilty for having a great time while knowing that I wasn't.

So as the weeks dragged on, and I heard from Jackson less and less often, I began to feel more and more isolated and alone. And even though I hated feeling this way and knew that I needed to get out and make more of an effort to meet new people, I couldn't seem to escape the heavy feeling of loneliness and despair.

The one thing I was looking forward to—the light at the end of the tunnel—was my upcoming nineteenth birthday in two weeks.

I had been excited about my birthday ever since I started planning it a few weeks ago. Jackson was taking the train down and Aunt Betty and Uncle Tom were driving into the city for the day. Even Charlie decided to take the week before Thanksgiving off so he could celebrate my birthday with me.

I had the whole day already planned out. We were going to spend the day at the Autumn's Colors and Chrysanthemum Festival at Longwood Gardens before heading to my birthday dinner at Vetri, an upscale Italian restaurant owned by the up-and-coming chef, Marc Vetri. I was so excited to see everyone, especially Jackson, and spend my birthday with those whom I loved and cared about. I knew having them around would make everything better. My birthday was exactly the thing I needed to get out of this slump.

***

November 21, 2003

Nineteen Years Old

My nineteenth birthday was today and it was turning out to be the worst birthday ever.

I woke up that morning with puffy, blood-shot eyes and a migraine. I had cried myself to sleep the night before. Luckily my roommate had left early for

Thanksgiving break and hadn't witnessed my complete mental breakdown.

I had cried because Jackson called me late the previous night.

I squealed in delight when I saw his name pop up on the screen when my phone started buzzing. It had been almost two weeks since we'd spoken on the phone. We'd both been busy with midterm exams and papers, but he had been even more busy because of his fraternity.

As I picked up to answer the phone, a wide grin spread across my face knowing that I was finally going to hear his voice.

But as soon as I did, I knew something was wrong.

"Hey, Clo." His voice was low, like he was whispering and didn't want anyone to hear him. But even through his muted voice, I could hear that he wasn't happy.

"Hey, Jax," I greeted him with apprehension, the excitement I'd felt just seconds ago gone from my voice. "How are you? I haven't talked to you in a while."

"I'm all right. How are you?"

"I'm good." I tried to sound cheerful as I braced myself for whatever he was about to say. "I really miss you. I'm really excited to see you tomorrow."

As soon as I finished my words, a sinking feeling crept its way into the pit of my stomach. This can't be about tomorrow, can it? I wanted to blurt out, "You're still coming, right?" but I held my tongue, afraid that if I asked that question out loud, I'd for sure make it come true.

"Clo…Please don't hate me…"

The sinking feeling in my stomach spread through my body. "What is it?" I finally managed to get out.

"I—I really hate to do this to you, but…I can't take the train down for your birthday tomorrow."

His words felt like a cold dagger through my heart.

"Why not?" I demanded, trying to keep my voice steady.

"I don't really have time to explain right now. I'm so sorry! I'm actually in the middle of a pledge activity. I snuck out real quick so I can tell you. I'm really, really sorry, Clo. I promise I'll make it up to you! You know I'd be there if I could." Then I heard a guy yelling in the background. "Shit! I gotta go, Clo. Please don't hate me. I'll call you tomorrow morning and will explain everything to you, okay?"

Before I could even respond, the line went silent, and he was already gone.

I got out of bed, feeling more tired that morning than I'd felt the previous night before bed. I looked out my dorm room window and saw that it had started snowing overnight and the pale, gray sky was filled with light flurries of snow drifting and swirling along with the wind. This was the first sign of snow this season, and I couldn't help but smile a little at how beautiful and peaceful the city looked while being blanketed by the first layer of white, powdery snow. It was one of my favorite things about the start of winter.

Just then I heard my phone beep, alerting me to a new text message. Feeling slightly better than when I'd initially woken up, I reached for my phone.

It was from Jackson and my spirits immediately brightened at the sight of his name. But then our conversation from the prior night hit my consciousness, deflating me once again. *Didn't he say he's going to call me this morning?*

Feeling a sense of dread, I pulled up his text message.

Happy birthday, Clo!!! I hope you have an amazing day! So sorry I can't make it! I was about to call you, but the brothers of the house just came unannounced and they're about to take my phone. I'll call you as soon as I can, but may not be until Sunday night. So sorry!!! Love, Jax

"You gotta be fucking kidding me," I blurted out loud as I stared at my phone in utter disbelief. In a crazed moment of anger, I pulled up his number and dialed it.

My call went straight to voicemail.

I slumped back onto my bed, feeling more upset than ever. How could Jackson do this to me? We always spent our birthdays together, and he'd promised he was going to come. How could he cancel on me in the last minute on my birthday for a frat house? How could he disregard my feelings like this?

There were so many feelings swirling inside me, I wasn't sure how I really felt. Anger? Disappointment? Sadness? Loneliness? Resentment? Betrayal? Abandonment? Was it possible for someone to feel all of these emotions all at once?

I crawled underneath my duvet, wishing I hadn't woken up that morning. How had a day I had been looking forward to for weeks turn out to be such a disappointment? At some point during my session of self-pity, I must have fallen back asleep, but the next thing I knew, the buzzing of my phone woke me up.

After a few seconds of fumbling through my sheets for the phone, I answered it quickly.

"Hi, Charlie." I was surprised to hear how awful my voice had just sounded.

"Happy birthday, kiddo!"

"Happy birthday, Chloe!" I heard Aunt Betty and Uncle Tom exclaim in the background.

"Thanks, guys." I tried to sound cheerful.

"Did we wake you? You sound out of it."

"Yeah, but it's okay. I must have drifted back to sleep, but I should get up now." I rubbed my eyes and drew in a deep breath. "So what time are you guys planning on coming over?" I looked over at my alarm clock on my nightstand and realized it was already close to ten in the morning.

"So that's why we called…" There was a short pause, and then some rustling.

"Hey, honey. It's me." It was Aunt Betty, who must have just grabbed the phone from Charlie.

"Hi, Aunt Betty. So what's wrong?" I held my breath, knowing it probably wasn't good news I was about to hear.

"Oh sweetie, have you taken a look outside this morning?"

I walked over to the window to see that the snow flurries I'd seen earlier were now larger snowflakes falling steadily from the sky.

"Yeah, it's snowing out." Then I realized what Aunt Betty was trying to say. "Do you think Longwood Gardens is closed today because of the snow?" Normally it didn't start snowing until the very last few days in November or early December, and Autumn's

Colors and Chrysanthemum Festival usually ended before the first snow fall.

"I'm not sure, honey, but that's very likely. That wasn't what we were concerned about."

"So what's the problem? It's just snow."

"The weather report this morning said that a large blizzard is currently moving through our area and staying until mid-day tomorrow. We're supposed to get about twenty-five to thirty inches of snow by tomorrow morning."

"Oh." I felt a sense of foreboding and I knew I didn't like where this was going. "So what does this mean for today?"

"Well, we were thinking maybe we can reschedule for maybe Sunday or next week. Charlie said he could look into getting everything rescheduled so you didn't have to do that."

"Reschedule? So you guys don't want to visit me?" I knew I sounded like a self-centered child at that moment, but after Jackson had flaked on me the night before, I wasn't sure I could handle my own family flaking on me as well.

"Would that be okay, honey?" I could hear the guilt in her voice. "I mean, it's just one option though," she quickly added. "I know you've been really excited about today, and today *is* your birthday. So if you feel strongly about celebrating today, just say the words and we'll come to pick you up and we can play it by ear and figure out something else to do instead of Longwood Gardens if they're closed. What do you think?"

I didn't need to think about it to know what I'd wanted for today. So for the first time that I could remember, I allowed my own selfish desires to take the front seat and told Aunt Betty what I wanted without holding back. "Aunt Betty, I really want to see you guys today. Jax canceled on me last night and won't be coming now. My birthday is today, not Sunday or next week. I don't really care what we end up doing today, but I just don't want to spend my birthday alone."

"Oh, honey. I'm so sorry to hear that about Jackson. We thought he might have taken the early train down this morning from Boston and was already with you. You're right, you shouldn't be alone for your birthday, and we're only forty minutes away. We can probably head out soon and be there in about an hour. Does that work?"

"That's perfect." I smiled, touched by how much she cared for me. "Thanks for understanding, Aunt Betty. I hope I didn't come off sounding ungrateful. I know I'm being selfish today. So it really means a lot to me that you guys are making the trip."

"Sweetie, don't be silly. You don't have a selfish bone in your body. I'm so glad that you're speaking up for what you want. You need to do that more often. You know we all love you. I wouldn't have even suggested postponing today if I had known Jackson wasn't there."

Her words brought tears to my eyes. "You guys are the best, Aunt Betty."

"So we'll see you in about an hour, then?"

"Yup. I'll see you guys then."

When I hung up the phone, I felt my mood improve. I was determined to make the best of my day. I wasn't going to let Jackson ruin my birthday because he decided it wasn't worth showing up for.

"Forget you, Jax," I said aloud. "I don't care that you can't come anymore. I'm going to have an amazing birthday without you because I'll be spending it with my family."

But I didn't end up having an amazing birthday after all. And I didn't end up spending it with Aunt Betty, Uncle Tom, or Charlie.

They never made it to my dorm that day. I waited almost five hours for their call, feeling increasingly agitated and concerned with every passing hour.

When I finally received the call, it wasn't from them.

It was from the hospital.

Chapter Nine

December 2003

Nineteen Years Old

Jackson

P ledging Alpha Sigma Delta had been brutally tough. They didn't call it Hell

Week for nothing and my grades and other obligations definitely suffered because of it. I had no time for anything else outside of pledging, not even Chloe.

Through all the sacrifice, sleepless nights, and humiliating things the brothers put me through, I was terrified I wouldn't make the cut. Nothing would be a bigger kick in the balls than if I'd gone through all this bullshit—and possibly upset Chloe in the process—for nothing.

But it hadn't been for nothing; and tonight, I officially crossed into the house and was now a brother of Alpha Sigma Delta. I couldn't wait to tell Chloe the great news the next time we talked.

After the initiation ceremony, it was tradition to celebrate with one hell of a party. It was like nothing I'd ever seen! Booze was everywhere and was thrown around like it was water. And like any crazy frat party, there were tons of hot girls. I'd had my share of girlfriends in high school, but these were college girls, and they were wild. Beautiful, sexy and very carefree with their bodies. It didn't take much encouragement before they started stripping in front of everyone.

It was funny though, as much as I was enjoying it all and basking in the glory of being in a frat house with all of its benefits, my thoughts kept going back to Chloe. The thought of her caused my stomach to twist in knots with guilt. I couldn't help but wonder what she was doing lately and if she was all right. We'd been virtually inseparable since the first grade, and now suddenly we were in separate cities going to different colleges six hours away from one another. I hated missing her so much and I sometimes wondered if she was as lonely and miserable as I was sometimes without her in my day-to-day life. Part of me wanted her to be happy, but mostly I hoped she was missing me too.

Other than a few quick text messages and emails, it'd been several weeks since we'd really had a chance to talk. I'd felt bad that I couldn't make it to Philly for her birthday the previous month. Between the two of us, it was the first birthday we hadn't spent together since we'd known each other. So I definitely felt bad that I broke our tradition because I got too busy. What made it worse was the fact that I'd promised Chloe that I'd be there. This was the first promise to her I'd broken. I felt like shit having to disappoint her the way I had, and I wondered if she was upset or maybe even mad at me for not being there for her when I'd said I would. I hoped, as my best friend, she'd understand and wouldn't be too upset. If she was, I hoped that she'd accept my apology once I had a chance to explain to her what'd happened.

When I started pledging the house over two months before, I had no clue what I'd signed up for. No one told me that pledging a fraternity would take up every waking moment of my day. I practically signed my life over to the fraternity and was a slave to their every beck and call.

So on the night before Chloe's birthday, when the brothers told my pledge class that there'd be a mandatory weekend "retreat" starting the following morning, I knew that I had to tell Chloe I couldn't make it for her birthday. By that point, I was over halfway through with the pledge period and had sacrificed too much to quit then. Plus, I really wanted to be a part of that frat house. The brothers all seemed really cool and I'd really bonded with the other pledges in my class. I knew that if I wanted the ultimate college experience, this would be the perfect group of guy friends to experience it with. But before that could happen, I had to pay my dues to become a brother of the house. And as a pledge, I was at the very bottom of the totem pole. So as much as I'd wanted to go see Chloe, by then I'd learned the hard way that missing any of the pledge activities was just not an option. Not only would I face a punishment, my entire pledge class would face one as well.

As I continued to think about Chloe, I realized that the last time we'd actually talked on the phone had been the night before her birthday when I had to tell her I couldn't make it. I remember receiving a few missed calls from her after that, but she never left a voicemail, which usually meant she was just calling to say hi but it wasn't anything important. I'd been meaning to call her back to see how she was doing.

Already buzzed from several shots I had just taken, I felt a strong urge to hear her voice. *I'll call her now!* Thinking that was a great idea, I pulled out my cell phone and looked for a place quiet enough to call her. The back porch seemed like the only place, and I headed for the back door.

"Hey, where are you going all by yourself?" A pretty, half-naked redhead cut me off before I could make my way out the door. She was clearly drunk as she eyed me up and down with a glazed-over expression on her face. She wrapped her arms around me, pressing her breasts against my body and slurred, "This frat house is just so *big*." She grabbed a hold of my crotch when she said "big" and I felt my cock twitch in a knee-jerk reaction. "Wanna show me upstairs and give me a private tour?" she whispered into my ear.

"Sorry, I can't right now," I slurred as I peeled her off of me and took a step back, almost losing my balance. "I need to call someone, and"—I stumbled forward and waved my finger at her—"you're not her."

"Oooooh! Gotta girlfriend?" She started to giggle as she leaned against the door frame for support. "I don't mind. Why don't you invite her to join us if you want?"

"Sorry, I'm not interested. And no, she's not my girlfriend. She's just my best friend."

The redhead laughed without humor. "So you're about to go call a girl who's just your *friend* when you're at a raging frat party and you're one of the guests of honor?" She scoffed. "Sounds like somebody's got a boner for a prude! She's not even your girlfriend and you're pining away for her like some pathetic loser."

"You have no idea what you're talking about." I wasn't sure why I felt the need to reason with her, but her words seemed to hit a nerve. Feeling annoyed, I tried to push past her to get to the back porch.

But she stopped me and grabbed my hand. "Forget her and let me show you a good time. You're young and you're in college. Now's the time to really live and have fun! Why are you pining after someone who's clearly not interested in you, or else she'd be here celebrating with you?"

Her comments pissed me off and I wanted to ditch her so I could call Chloe. Suddenly, one of my new frat brothers, Tyler, came up from behind and slapped me heartily on the back. He shoved a tall glass filled with a strange murky-colored liquid into my hand. "Yo, man, taste this shit! It'll give you a killer buzz!"

"I'm game!" The redhead grabbed the glass from me and took a swig before I could stop her. She handed it back to Tyler who drank about half of it before passing the glass back to me. I didn't want to look like a dud in front of my new frat bro, so I took the glass and gulped down the rest.

It smelled terrible and tasted even worse. "What was that shit?" I coughed and tried not to gag.

He shrugged. "Who knows? Who cares? Kyle made it in the chem lab when the professor wasn't watching!" Tyler laughed.

Tyler wasn't joking, the homemade brew hit me hard and the room was already starting to spin. And when my cell phone in my hand started to ring, I had forgotten I was even holding it.

Before I could step away to answer the call, Tyler grabbed the phone from my hand and looked at the screen. "Who's Chloe Sinclair?"

The redhead between us cackled. "That must be the non-girlfriend he's pining over! Let me guess, she calls and you come running like a love-sick puppy? Meanwhile she's not even putting out for you. Am I right?"

I knew this crazy girl's words weren't true, but it was hard to not let them affect me. "It's not like that," I said through gritted teeth as I tried to grab my phone back from Tyler.

Tyler laughed as he stumbled back a step to avoid my reach. "Dude, I think this chick's right. You're whipped, aren't you?"

"Come on, bro." Even in my drunken haze, I knew reasoning with someone who was clearly wasted was pointless.

"Let me talk to her. I'll tell her you've found a real woman who can actually fuck!" The redhead took the phone from Tyler and before I could stop her, she pressed answer.

In a state of panic, I finally grabbed the phone from them, but they had already hit answer and I could hear Chloe's voice coming through the line.

"Hello? Jax?"

"Hey. Yeah, it's me. What's up?" I tried to play it cool.

"Are you free to talk? Something's happened recently, and it's all my fault. I really need you right now." Her words came out in the tremble.

As the room started to sway around me, I couldn't quite understand what she was talking about, but I felt like something was wrong. She sounded so fragile and vulnerable. All I wanted to do was go to her and hold her and tell her everything was going to be okay.

But I couldn't. My body stopped listening to me. The alcohol inside me had worked its way through my system and I was feeling really sick. I dropped to the floor to sit down, hoping it'd stop the room from moving so much. As my head swirled, I knew there was no way I could go anywhere. I also knew there was no way I was going to get up from this floor anytime soon.

I wanted to say something to comfort Chloe, but I noticed that Tyler and the redhead had attracted a crowd from the party and they were all listening in now.

"Hello? Jax, did you even hear what I said?"

"Yeah, I heard. I'm so sorry, Clo. I wish I was there for you." Then I heard all the snickering and laughter from the crowd. "But listen, I can't really talk right now. Can I call you tomorrow morning?"

"Oooohhh! Can I call you tomorrow morning?" a number of the guys from the crowd chanted sarcastically. To them it was all a game, but I could tell Chloe was really hurting. If only I could focus and think through the fog, if only I could get up and find a way to get to her, then maybe I'd know what I could say to comfort her right then.

"I guess so." Her voice was barely audible and then the line went dead.

I wanted to call her right back because I knew that I had somehow upset her. But instead, my body felt heavy and I sprawled onto the floor. As I drifted in and out of consciousness, the crowd standing over me laughing, slowly disappeared and all my thoughts went to Chloe. There was a nagging feeling that pricked at my insides, and I had an odd feeling that she wasn't okay. *I'll call her first thing tomorrow morning. She's my best friend and I need to be there for her.* That was the last thought that went through my mind right before I finally passed out.

***

But I didn't call her the next morning.

When I woke up the next morning on one of the couches in the frat house, I immediately leaped up when I saw the time on my phone. I raced out of the door, hoping I could get back to my dorm room to grab my backpack and then make it to my Econ. 101 class before it started fifteen minutes later. I knew I couldn't miss any more classes that semester or I might fail out. With everything that was happening between my parents and their divorce, I didn't want to stress my mom out more if I flunked out of Harvard after just one semester.

But in my rush to get to class, I'd accidentally left my cell phone behind at the frat house. By the time I finished my last class of the day and returned to the frat house to pick it up, another party was already in full swing. Luckily everyone was out in the other room playing beer pong, and I found my phone where I'd left it on the mantel of my fireplace next to the couch. I cringed with guilt when I switched on my cell phone and saw that I'd received several missed texts from Chloe.

I quickly shot a text back to her.

> **Me:** Hey Clo. Sorry, I left my phone at the frat house all day and just got it now and saw your texts. You okay?

To my surprise, Chloe texted me right back.

> **Chloe:** Hi Jax. A lot has been going on and I need to talk to you about it.
>
> **Me:** Sorry I've been MIA. I finally crossed into the frat, so I'll be more free now b/c I'm not a pledge anymore. What's wrong? Talk about what?

> **Chloe:** That's great Jax. I know getting into the frat was important. I haven't said anything b/c I wanna tell you over the phone. I also didn't want to bother you if you were busy.
>
> **Me:** I'm not busy. I can call you now, if you want.

I was feeling a tinge of guilt grow inside me as I texted back and forth with Chloe. It seemed like something serious was going on with her that she'd been waiting to tell me.

Then another text came through from her:

> **Chloe:** I'm about to get off work in 15 mins. Should be home in 30 and can talk any time after that.
>
> **Me:** Okay. I'll call you in 30. :)

As I put away my phone and made a mental note to call Chloe at six-thirty, I wondered why she hadn't mentioned she had a job. *I'll ask her when I call her in a bit.*

Before I could think about it for any longer, I saw Tyler and the redhead from the night before walking toward me. It was clear from the way the girl had her arms around Tyler that they'd hooked up.

"Hey, Jackson! We're having a beer pong competition in the next room. Up for a round against me?" Tyler asked. "Jill, here, wants to see if I can beat you." He shot me a look and I could tell he wanted to impress the girl.

I wanted to turn them down, go back to my dorm, and call Chloe, but I knew that if I backed down from a beer pong challenge on my first full day of being a brother in the house, I'd never hear the end of it. I sized up the competition, and I could tell Tyler was already well on his way to being drunk. I was completely sober and was pretty good at beer pong. I knew it wouldn't take long to beat Tyler and sneak out afterward. My dorm was only a five-minute walk from there, so I knew that I had plenty of time before Chloe was free to talk.

"You're on, bro. I'm always game to kick some ass." I flashed them a competitive smirk as I followed them to the other room where a round of beer pong was already in progress.

Before I knew it, three hours had flown by, and I was laughing and having the time of my life as the new beer pong champion of Alpha Sigma Delta house. I had a crown made of aluminum foil on my head, a blonde on one arm and Jill, the redhead, on the other. I felt like I was on top of the world as the whole house chanted my name in victory.

It wasn't until I woke up the next morning in one of the extra bedrooms in the house that I realized I had never called Chloe like I'd said I would. I rubbed my forehead, feeling like shit. I was officially the worst friend ever. I looked over to the blonde and the redhead who were both naked in the bed with me, stinking of alcohol.

Fuck! How did things get so out of hand last night? I had to squirm out from under both girls to get out of the bed. I looked around the room for my cell phone but couldn't find it anywhere.

"What the fuck is wrong with me? This is the second time in twenty-four hours." Feeling annoyed, I threw on my clothes and went downstairs, hoping I had left my phone in the room where the beer pong competition had taken place. To my relief, it was there under the beer pong table.

I immediately groaned when I saw how many missed calls and texts I had received from Chloe. I punched the wall with my bare fist in frustration and anger at myself. "I'm the shittiest friend in the world!"

As I scrolled through my missed call log, I noticed that one of her calls the night before—the last one she'd made to me at a little after ten—had been answered and the call had lasted almost half a minute. But I had no memory of this call or what we'd talked about.

Anxiety churned in the pit of my stomach as I quickly grabbed my stuff and headed back to my dorm. I knew I needed to talk to Chloe today, and this time, I needed to make sure I was sober and away from any distractions.

Chapter Ten

December 2003

Nineteen Years Old

Chloe

During the last two weeks since my nineteenth birthday, anything and everything that could have gone wrong, had. Jackson broke his promise to visit that weekend. A crazy blizzard hit the area on the morning of my birthday, but because I didn't want to be alone, I guilt-tripped Aunt Betty, Uncle Tom, and Charlie to drive into the city to spend the day with me. I knew the roads would be a mess because of the snowstorm. I knew I was putting them at risk. But at that moment in time, I hadn't cared. It was my birthday, and I was more lonely that day than I'd ever been before. I'd convinced myself that it was okay to be selfish just that one time, that we'd experienced and driven through worse blizzards than that one so nothing would go wrong.

But of course, fate proved me wrong.

On their way to see me that day, they were going too fast on the icy roads, lost control of their car, and crashed into a tree. Aunt Betty and Uncle Tom both sustained several broken bones and some cuts and bruises, but nothing too serious. But Charlie had been driving and didn't have his seatbelt on. When the car had hit the tree, his body was thrown forward through the windshield, and he sustained severe injuries.

During the past two weeks since the accident, Charlie had had to undergo a number of surgeries, and today was his latest surgery where they'd go in and take a look at his spinal cord. Aunt Betty had been texting me throughout the day to update me on the status of the all-day surgery. After my morning shift at McDonald's, one of my two new part-time jobs I'd picked up the previous week to help with some of the hospital bills, I rushed back to the hospital to be there when the surgery was over.

After ten hours of surgery, one of the surgeons came out to talk to us. Despite the odds, we were still hopeful, and prayed for a miracle that we'd receive some good news.

But we didn't.

Instead, the surgeon said the words we'd been dreading all along: "We had to go in and insert rods and plates along his spine to help stabilize it. Unfortunately, we were also able to confirm that your son's spinal cord was indeed severed during the accident. As a result, he's lost all motor function from the waist down, and he won't be able to walk again. I'm very sorry."

"No!" Aunt Betty let out a hysterical wail as she collapsed against me, sobbing like I'd never seen her sob before.

My eyes full of tears, I tried to comfort her as she continued to cry in my arms. "I'm so sorry," I kept repeating as I stroked her back.

Grief-stricken, Uncle Tom fell back onto one of the chairs in the waiting room. He hunched over and buried his face in his hands. He didn't make a sound, but I could see his body move up and down as he wept into his hands in silence.

Even though the doctors tried to prepare us for this outcome, the news was just as devastating and hit us hard.

This was all my fault, and the immense guilt I carried inside only deepened the hurt I felt from hearing the news. I had done this to Charlie and he didn't deserve this. Aunt Betty didn't deserve this. Uncle Tom didn't deserve this.

Charlie had always been like a brother to me, accepting me into his family even though I had taken over his room and a big portion of his parents' time and energy. He'd never complained or resented me. Instead, he treated me like his equal and spoiled me whenever he'd visit for the holidays. So hearing the news that he was permanently paralyzed from the waist down for the rest of his life left me feeling empty and numb with anguish.

But I didn't deserve to be comforted by Aunt Betty and Uncle Tom. Their only son—the young, successful lawyer they were so proud of—had just had the rest of his life ruined because of me, because of my selfishness, because of my inability to love someone without them getting hurt.

While I didn't deserve it, I still couldn't help but want to be comforted. I still wanted someone there to tell me everything would be okay. I still wanted someone to tell me that I wasn't an awful person. I still wanted someone to tell me that it wasn't my fault, even when I knew that wasn't true.

Jackson was the only person who I could talk to about this. He was the only person who could comfort me. Since my birthday, I'd tried to call him a number of times, to tell him what happened, to hear his warm, familiar voice. But every time I called, he was never there to pick up.

A part of me was mad at Jackson for neglecting me and not being there for me. But another part of me—the part that increased with each passing day that I didn't hear from him—was worried sick that something had happened to him. With everything that'd happened recently, and everything that'd happened with my mom, I was terrified to imagine possibly losing him as well.

So on my way back to my dorm from the hospital, I decided to try calling Jackson again. I heard the phone ring several times, and on the fifth ring, I knew I'd get voicemail again and was about to end the call. But just as I was about to switch off, I heard a click.

I put the phone back to my ear, but instead of Jackson's voice, all I heard was the rustling of fabric against the phone and what seemed like a loud party in the distant background.

"Hello? Jax?"

I heard a sudden movement and then, to my surprise, Jackson's voice.

"Hey. Yeah, it's me. What's up?" His words were abrupt but slurred, and it was clear to me that he was drunk.

"Are you free to talk? Something's happened recently, and it's all my fault. I really need you right now." The words flooded out of me in a trembling rush.

I expected him to say something right away, to ask me what was wrong, to console me in his own special way. But after a long period of time, I heard nothing but his heavy breathing, the party in the background, and the rustling sound of the phone being brushed up against something.

Feeling my irritation rise, I finally tried again. "Hello? Jax, did you even hear what I said?"

"Yeah, I heard," he said flatly, almost defensively. "I'm so sorry, Clo. I wish I was there for you."

I felt my irritation subside at his words. I desperately wished he was here too. But then I heard a crowd of laughter growing louder in the background. Jackson quickly continued, "But listen, I can't really talk right now. Can I call you tomorrow morning?"

Then I heard a crowd of people repeat, "Oooohhh! Can I call you tomorrow morning?" before breaking off into laughter.

"I guess so," I managed to say, trying so hard to hold back the tears. Then I hung up on him. A sudden pain pierced through my chest. I knew I should be relieved that he was okay—and alive—but I didn't feel relieved. I felt hurt—especially because the real reason he wasn't returning my calls wasn't because he was busy with his classes. It was because he was busy having fun with his fraternity and getting drunk at parties.

In spite of my hurt, I still wanted to talk to Jackson. I still missed him deeply. So I waited for his call the next morning.

But the call never came. By one o'clock in the afternoon, when I left my second part-time job at Starbucks, he still hadn't called or texted.

At this point, I felt my patience reach its limit and I sent him a text. Then another an hour later. And yet another two hours after that. Still nothing.

It wasn't until six o'clock, when I was closing out of my register at McDonald's, that I'd finally heard from him. After a few text message exchanges, he said he'll call me in half an hour.

I tried not to be hopeful, but when I arrived back to my dorm room, I couldn't help but feel the anticipation of finally having a conversation with him.

But then six-thirty passed, and he didn't call. I texted him to see if he was still planning on calling.

When I hadn't heard from him by seven o'clock, I shot him a text message and tried calling him. Still nothing.

When eight rolled around, I texted again. Silence.

At some point into the night, I had fallen asleep on my bed on top of the duvet. It wasn't until ten that I woke up and realized I'd fallen asleep, waiting for him. I looked at my phone hopefully but was disappointed to see nothing new from Jackson.

Feeling frustrated and emotionally exhausted, I pulled up his number and dialed it. His voicemail picked up.

As frustration turned into anger, I dialed his number two more times, thinking at some point, he would have to pick up.

Finally, on my fourth attempt, someone picked up.

"Hello?" a guy yelled into the phone. I could hear loud music and people talking and laughing in the background.

"Hi! Is Jackson there?" I screamed into the phone, hoping he could hear me.

"Who?"

"Jackson! Jackson Pierce! You just picked up Jackson's phone!"

"Ahh, yeah, my boy, Jackson!" Then I heard him chuckle.

"Can you get him for me?"

"Sorry. No can do. He's in the middle of some fun. I'm not going to cock-block. You know, bro code and all."

"What are you talking about? What is he doing?" I knew what the answer was, but the masochist in me still wanted to hear it for myself.

"Jeez, do I need to spell it out for you? He's up in some room fucking two hot broads right now." He laughed again. "And let me tell you, that wild redhead is our resident slut on Greek row. She's definitely going to show him and the blonde a fucking wild time tonight. He's going to have so much pussy tonight, let's hope his dick doesn't fall off."

"Hey, Tyler!" I heard someone scream in the background, "Get off the fuckin' phone! We're all shot-gunning some beers here."

"Sorry. Gotta go," the guy, who I assumed was Tyler, said quickly before the phone went silent.

Chapter Eleven

December 2003

Nineteen Years Old

Chloe

Half an hour later, I strode into the closest bar to my dorm, determined to have fun and cut loose. *Forget you, Jackson!* He wasn't the only one who knew how to get drunk and have fun. Tonight, I felt reckless and I wanted to hurt Jackson the way he'd hurt me.

I was wearing my hottest little black dress; cut low in the front and high on the thigh. I put on extra makeup tonight, hoping I could trick the bartender into thinking I was at least twenty-one so he wouldn't ask for my ID.

I sat on the stool at the end of the bar, trying to look like I belonged. The bartender pointedly drummed his fingers on the sign that read, *Customers must be twenty-one to purchase alcohol,* and I knew I was busted.

"Can I help you with something?" the bartender asked with a knowing edge to his voice.

"No thanks, I'm just here to meet someone," I bluffed, jutting out my chin to show I wasn't intimidated, even though I knew I was about be thrown out on my ass and humiliated in front of everyone.

Then a man sitting alone at a nearby table came over and smiled at me. "I believe you're waiting for me. Hi, I'm Michael Davison."

"Michael! I've really been looking forward to meeting you face to face!" I smiled brightly as he acted like a mutual friend had arranged for us to meet.

His lie of a blind date was the perfect cover and I was grateful for his willingness to help me out in this embarrassing situation.

"Can I buy you a drink?" Michael asked. He was a cute guy with handsome features. He was wearing a very expensive suit and looked like a successful businessman. Maybe he was visiting Philly on a business trip. He looked like he was in his early thirties and from the way he eyed me up and down, I knew that he was looking for a good time that night.

He's perfect for what I want tonight, I thought to myself as I actively forced out thoughts of Jackson.

I glanced at the bartender who was still eying me suspiciously, and then turned back to Michael. "What do you say we get that drink someplace else?"

"Sure." He flashed me a devious smile. "I'm staying in the hotel across the street. We could go there if you want."

I wasn't a virgin, but I wasn't a girl who went to hotel rooms with strange men, either. I knew nothing about this man. He could be married, or a criminal, or worse. *Maybe I should just go home and go to bed.*

Suddenly I realized this was just the sort of worrying that Jackson always said I did too much of. I had gone out tonight to let loose and remind myself that I was single, that I shouldn't be waiting by the phone for my best friend to call, that I had a life of my own. Tonight, I needed to have some mindless, uncomplicated fun, and that's exactly what this stranger could offer me.

I flashed Michael my sexiest smile and bit my lower lip. "Sounds good to me."

His hotel was very nice, complete with a doorman at the front of the hotel and gorgeously arranged bouquets in antique Victorian vases on all the tables in the lobby. I shifted uncomfortably in my outfit, feeling distinctly out of place in my slutty dress and darkly-drawn eyeliner. I followed him quickly through the lobby, up the elevator, and into his hotel suite.

"Make yourself comfortable and I'll have room service bring up some drinks," he said as he picked up the hotel phone and called down for a bottle of vodka and a bottle of Bacardi 151.

I considered sitting on the edge of the giant, king-sized bed in the center of the room, but I quickly stopped myself, realizing how bold that'd be, and also how very unlike me that'd be. So I opted instead to sit on the sofa situated against the far wall.

The hem of my dress moved dangerously higher when I sat down. I caught Michael's eyes looking at the exposed skin when I sat down as he walked over with the tray of Bacardi and vodka. He joined me on the cushion beside mine and set the tray on an end table. As he poured us each a shot of the drinks, I felt nervous about having hard liquor for the first time.

Think about Jackson. He's sure enjoying himself with alcohol, a voice inside me said encouragingly.

I drew in a deep breath and realized there was no way I was backing down now.

I clinked my shot glass of Bacardi 151 to his and said, "To a fun night!"

"To a fun night!" he agreed and we both downed our shots.

I'd never had anything stronger than beer before and wasn't prepared for the difference. The Bacardi burned my throat and I thought I was going to die. Desperate to soothe the fire, I grabbed the vodka and gulped down the clear liquid that looked like water. But I discovered quickly that was clearly a mistake, and it was nothing like water.

Michael grabbed me a bottle of water from the mini fridge and offered it to me, but I shook my head, determined to try to act cool and collected. "No thanks; I'm fine."

"Oh, you're more than fine," he said as his lips twisted into a smile. The meaning of his words were clear as he looked me up and down with lust burning in his eyes.

I blushed and my face grew hot, and I wondered if this was the effects of the alcohol. I smiled at Michael, feeling sexy, empowered, and uninhibited all of a sudden. "So, tell me about yourself, Michael Davison. Who are you?" I asked seductively as I leaned forward into him.

To my surprise, Michael handed me his business card and I whistled loudly to show how impressed I was. He was a lawyer from a big firm in New York City.

"And what brings you to Philly?" I flirted shamelessly, crossing and uncrossing my legs like I'd seen women do in the movies. It had just the effect that I was hoping for as I saw a bulge growing in his slacks.

"I'm here just for the week, taking depositions from witnesses for a case we've been working on." He shifted uncomfortably on the couch, trying to adjust himself.

"That sounds fascinating! You must be extremely smart to be a lawyer."

"Ah, it's not as exciting as it sounds." Michael shrugged off the compliment, but I could tell he was eating it up. He was grinning from ear to ear and poured us another round of shots. As he handed me a shot, he leaned in and whispered in my ear, "I'm more interested in you."

"What do you want to know?" I gulped down another shot of Bacardi and then one of vodka. They went down easier the second time, and I felt myself buzzing hard. To my surprise, the alcohol had made me feel relaxed, happy, and incredibly horny.

Michael looked at me. "You're the sexiest woman I've ever met, and I don't even know your name." I watched as his eyes moved down my neck and stopped on my breasts.

"Well, I can fix that." I took the hotel notepad from the nearby end table and folded it into a business card, seductively running the paper through my fingers as I made fuck-me eyes at him over the edge. Then I wrote my name and phone number on it and handed it to him formally, like we were business partners.

"I see. Well I'm glad to meet you, Chloe." He grinned and tucked the paper into his jacket pocket. "So what do you want to do tonight? Anywhere in the city you wanna check out tonight?"

My body was on fire at this point from all the alcohol and all I wanted to do was release all the pent-up energy and stress I'd felt for the past few weeks. "Michael," I said his name slowly as I licked my lower lip, "I think we should just stay in and make our own fun."

Then I moved toward him like a cat preparing to pounce on its prey. The second round of shots had definitely lowered my inhibitions, and my need to prove to myself that I could have fun like Jackson fueled me on. I was going to fuck this stranger tonight, and I was going to enjoy it.

I lunged at him, pushing him back against the hotel sofa and pulling off his pants. His erection immediately sprang free and I took him greedily into my mouth, not waiting another second. I was determined to give him the best blowjob he'd ever had and took him deeply into my throat while I cradled his balls.

"Oh my God," he groaned. He pushed his cock deeper into my mouth as he ran his hands through my hair, encouraging me on. "This is amazing, Chloe!"

Seconds later, he began to spasm and I knew he was near his climax. I pulled him from my mouth and did a sexy striptease for him so he could have a moment to cool down. I wasn't ready for him to be done just yet.

Michael gawked in awe as I peeled the dress from my body and began to caress my naked skin with my hands. His eyes grew wide as he watched my hands move down between my inner thighs as I began to pleasure myself, masturbating in front of him while he began to stroke his cock.

"You are making me so hot! I can't wait to feel me inside you!" he panted as he grabbed a condom from the nightstand and put it on. I saw little beads of sweat glistening on his forehead and I knew he was more than ready for me.

"Well, let's not wait, then," I countered as I straddled him on the couch, enveloping his cock with my eager, wet folds.

"Fuck!" he roared out in pleasure as I took in the entire length of his shaft. "You are the hottest woman I've ever met. You're so tight, and wet, and gorgeous!" Michael groaned as I thrust wildly on top of him, fueled by the need to escape my own problems and to prove to myself that I could have meaningless sex.

My body reacted to the physical stimulation and it began to feel good; really good! It didn't take long before I orgasmed loudly on top of him, crying out as every muscle and nerve in my body surged with pleasure.

Michael's eyes rolled back and he groaned as he reached his own climax.

We did it twice more that night, once in the shower and once in the bed before finally falling into a deep and drunken sleep.

When I awoke the next morning, my head was pounding and I felt sick to my stomach. It took me a moment to recognize my strange surroundings, and when I did, I felt even worse.

What was I thinking last night? Was it worth demeaning myself with some stranger just to show up Jackson? I realized that I had to get out of there and talk to Jackson. I didn't care if he was busy. This was ridiculous and I needed to see him.

I'd never had a one-night stand before, or anything remotely dirty like that, and I wasn't sure what I was supposed to do before I left.

I turned toward him on the bed and whispered. "Thanks for last night, Michael, but I'm afraid I've got to go."

When he didn't respond, I tried shaking him. That was when I realized the body sleeping beside me was actually a pile of pillows under the sheets.

I sat up on the bed and realized that Michael was already gone. Then something on the nightstand caught my attention.

It was an unmarked envelope.

Confused, I picked it up and opened it, expecting to find some kind of goodbye note. But to my surprise, it was filled with hundred-dollar bills. Thirty of them to be exact. It was three thousand dollars in cash.

"Holy shit!" I exclaimed, and the loudness of my own voice made my head want to explode. I don't think I'd ever been so hung over.

This didn't make sense. Why did Michael leave me money? There must be some explanation for the money. Some detail that I'd missed because my head hurt so badly.

Then I turned the envelope upside down and a piece of paper fell out of it. It was a business card that read Madam Celine's Escort Service; attractive companionship for the busy professional male. Always Discreet, Always Satisfying. Client Cums First.

"Oh my God! He thought I was an escort," I gasped. And just like that, I felt more sick at that moment than I'd felt all morning, and I immediately ran into the bathroom and vomited until there was nothing left in my stomach.

Afterward, I should have felt better, but I didn't. *How could he have thought I was an escort?* I thought back to the previous night and tried to remember all the things he'd said and done, and all the things I'd said and done in return. As each embarrassing scene from the night before came into focus, it all became horribly clear: he'd gone to the bar to meet up with an escort and when I said I was waiting for someone, he'd mistaken me for the escort he was meant to meet.

I riffled through the room until I found the business card he had given me. I needed to give him the money back. I felt dirty just being in the same room as that envelope full of cash. I dialed the number on Michael's business card and got a receptionist at the law firm. When she offered to take a message, I hung up the phone as fast as I could, mortified beyond words at the idea of leaving a message for someone who just paid for my body. *What do you even say to such a guy? "Hey, remember me? Well, I'm not an escort, I'm just a slut. Call me back so I can return your three grand. Thanks."*

I reached for the envelope and looked at the cash again. Maybe I should give the money to the police or donate it to a charity? *Aunt Betty and Uncle Tom could sure use some charity right now.* I quickly pushed that thought from my mind. No, that would be completely wrong to keep the money and give it to them. That would basically be turning myself into an escort.

And I was not an escort. This was just a mistake. I'd been looking for a one-night stand and it was just a misunderstanding. If I intentionally kept the money now, it wouldn't be a mistake any longer; it would be prostitution.

Chapter Twelve

December 2003

Nineteen Years Old

Chloe

I realized that I needed to sort this whole mess out somewhere I felt comfortable and safe. I decided to take a trip back home to see Aunt Betty and Uncle Tom.

The forty-minute drive helped. I kept the window down and the cold air hitting my face helped wash away my hangover and clear my head. By the time I got there, I felt almost human again.

But then I gasped when I saw it. As I pulled up into the driveway, there was a new "For Sale" sign in the front yard.

"Hi, sweetie. What an unexpected surprise. Is everything okay at school?" Aunt Betty folded me into her arms in a motherly embrace.

I looked over into the living room and was surprised to see Uncle Tom passed out in his recliner. There was a half-empty bottle of whiskey and a dirty, empty glass on the side table next to his recliner. From the smell of alcohol that lingered in the air, I had a feeling he'd drunk more than enough to get himself drunk.

"School's fine." I paused, unsure how to bring up the subject. "Aunt Betty, why is there a For Sale sign in the front yard?" I decided not to beat around the bush.

Aunt Betty looked down at her hands so I wouldn't see the tears brimming in her eyes. "This house has just gotten too big for us now that you've gone off to school."

I knew this wasn't the real reason. "Come on, Aunt Betty. I know how much you love this house. There are so many great memories that happened in this house. I know you guys would never put it up for sale because you thought it was too big. Please tell me what's really going on?"

She let out a heavy sigh. "You're right, honey. There's no point hiding the truth from you." She met my gaze and I noticed how bloodshot and sunken-in her eyes were, and I immediately felt the guilt that'd become a constant gnaw against my insides. "Our insurance didn't cover all of Charlie's medicals bills. Some of the surgeries weren't covered. The doctors also told us that Charlie's recovery process from the accident will be a lengthy one. He'll need to stay in the hospital for some time and he may need continuous physical therapy for a number of years so he can adjust to…"

She couldn't finish the sentence, but I knew what she was going to say and a lump formed in the back of my throat. "Are you sure there isn't another way? Selling the house just seems so final."

Her shoulder slumped and her eyes filled with tears. She shook her head. "I don't think so, honey. I just don't know how we can manage it all without giving up the house. Even if we sell a lot of our things and refinance the house, it won't be enough. Based on what we're anticipating, we'll need at least half a million dollars to pay for all the medical bills in the first year. Even if we were to withdraw early from our retirement funds, we don't have enough money saved to cover everything. Tom's worried that we'll have to file for bankruptcy." Her words broke into a sob as she buried her face in her hands.

"Oh, Aunt Betty, I'm so sorry." I held her tightly as she cried helplessly in my arms. The only other time

I'd seen her cry was when my mom had passed away, and this felt worse than that because I knew it was all my fault. "I wish none of this ever happened." I wanted to tell her that it was all my fault, that I wished it'd been me in the car instead, that I'd gladly take his place right now if I could so he could continue living his normal life before the accident. That was how I felt.

But I couldn't voice any of those thoughts to her, or to Uncle Tom. I knew them well enough to know that they'd just console me and tell me that I shouldn't think that way, that I had done nothing wrong, that it was no one's fault. And as much as I wanted to hear those words, they were the last two people who should tell me that it hadn't been my fault, that I hadn't done anything wrong.

"If we sell the house, your uncle and I can move into a small apartment. The utilities will be cheaper and we'll be able to use the money to pay off some of the medical expenses that we've incurred. Then we hope we can pay for Charlie's ongoing physical therapy with our combined income after our monthly expenses." She sighed. "I think that's the best plan we've got."

Then something occurred to me.

"Aunt Betty, you, Uncle Tom, and Charlie have loved me, taken care of me, and provided me with so much. I want to help out as much as I can. I owe you guys at least that." With my heart in my throat, I reached into my purse and pulled out the three thousand dollars that was stuffed inside and handed it to her. "I came to give you this. Maybe it'll cover some of the expenses for now. I have another two thousand dollars in my savings that I'll bring over later this week."

She gasped aloud and hugged me so tight I could hardly breathe. Fresh tears of relief flowed down her cheeks and made me wet too. "This is a miracle. This will save us for another month. But where did you get this much money?"

"I've been saving it from my two part-time jobs."

I expected her to question me further. She knew I had just started those two jobs shortly after the accident a few weeks before. But to my surprise, she didn't. Maybe with all the stress, it hadn't crossed her mind. Or maybe she was at a point where she'd believe anything if it'd help make life just a little easier.

When she took the money from me, there was a wave of relief and hope on her face that touched my heart. It felt amazing to be able to give back to the woman who had loved and raised me like I was her own child. And at that moment, it didn't even bother me to know where that money had come from.

***

That evening after dinner, as I lay in the room that had been both mine and Charlie's at different periods of time, I thought back to all the precious memories I'd had in this room. I thought about how happy my life had been while living in this house. With each memory I recalled, I realized more and more how emotionally attached I'd become to this bedroom, to this house. I couldn't imagine having to say goodbye to it all.

Just then, my phone rang, and to my surprise, it was the ever-elusive Jackson.

For a brief second, I thought about ignoring his call—to give him a taste of his own medicine—but as the phone continued to ring, I gave in and answered.

"Hi," I said plainly, torn between being angry at him and missing him.

"Hey, Clo. I'm so sorry for not calling you back sooner. It's just been a really crazy month with pledging and everything. I hope you're not mad."

"Do you want the truth, or do you want me to tell you I'm not mad?" I asked him bluntly, giving him the answer passive aggressively.

"I deserved that." Jackson's voice was filled with agony. "You have every reason to be upset with me. Clo, I know I've been a really shitty friend to you in the past few weeks. You deserve better. You've always been there for me, even when I pushed you away. I should have been there for you when you needed me. I hope you can forgive me."

I was silent and tears welled up in my eyes as I listened to his apology. While a part of me wanted to stay angry with him, I knew it wasn't worth our friendship. I had been upset with Jackson for breaking his promise to visit me for my birthday. I had been upset with him for neglecting me and not returning my calls or texts. But what was the point in staying angry with him after he'd just apologized? What else did I want him to do? Not enjoy his time in college? Not date girls but stay single and miserable? Not be out having fun, getting drunk, and being happy? None of that would make sense. He was my best friend. It wasn't his fault that I hadn't made many friends in college. It wasn't his fault that I felt lonely and miserable. And it definitely wasn't his fault that I felt guilty for ruining the rest of Charlie's life and causing Aunt Betty and Uncle Tom to sell their house.

Mistaking my silence for anger, Jackson continued, "Clo, I know I don't deserve your forgiveness. I broke my promise and stood you up on your birthday. I really feel awful about that. I never called you or texted you back when I promised I would. And even when you told me that you needed to talk to me because something was wrong, I still didn't give you the time and attention you needed and deserved. I've been the worst friend to you, and I'm really sorry. I—"

"Jax," I said, finally cutting him off. "You don't have to explain. I know you're just enjoying your freshman year, and I'm really happy to know that everything's been going well for you. But the problem is, things haven't been going well for me recently, and you haven't been around to be my best friend to even know anything that's been happening. So even though I'm upset that you didn't show up to my birthday, what I'm more upset about is the fact that you haven't been around for me to even talk to. I really needed a friend during the past few weeks and you weren't there."

"Clo...I don't even know what to say. I'm a fucking asshole and I treated you like shit. I've just been so caught up with everything with the fraternity and being in college, I completely took you for granted and neglected our friendship. I'm so sorry. You needed me and I wasn't there for you. But if you can forgive me for being such a dumbass, can you tell me now what's been happening? I'm all ears."

My lips curled into a small smile as I considered making Jackson squirm and grovel a little bit longer. But my need to tell him about Charlie and the all-consuming guilt I'd felt won out.

So I told him about what happened on my birthday, about the blizzard, about Aunt Betty's suggestion that we'd reschedule due to the bad weather, about how I guilt-tripped them to come see me anyway, and about the accident and Charlie's resulting paralysis.

When I got to the part about Charlie, Jackson interrupted my story. "Clo, that's not your fault. You couldn't have known any of that was going to happen. You can't blame yourself for everything. You can't think that any of this is your fault, because it's not."

Tears fell down my face as I finally heard what I'd been waiting to hear from him. "But if it wasn't for me, it wouldn't have happened…"

"Clo, don't do this to yourself. If you use that kind of logic, you can say it was my fault for standing you up that caused you to insist that they drive to see you that day; you can say it was Aunt Betty's fault for not being more firm about not traveling because of the weather; you can even say it was Charlie's fault for not wearing a seatbelt and not being more careful while driving." He sighed. "What I'm trying to say is, we can spend all day blaming someone for what happened, but the truth is, bad things happen and we can't predict the future to know what will happen next. You can't beat yourself up over something you didn't want to happen."

"Thanks, Jax…I really needed that." I wished he were there with me at that very moment. I wished he were just next door like old times so I could go see him and give him a hug.

Then the events of the night before flashed before my eyes and I cringed at the thought of what I had done. "Jax, so something happened last night." I suddenly felt nervous about admitting to it.

"What is it?" I could hear the anxiety in his voice.

"So I was really upset last night and I went out and...I met a guy, and we had a little too much to drink...and we ended up hooking up and..."

"Clo, can I stop you right there?" he said, cutting me off.

"Uh. Okay?" I wasn't sure why he interrupted me. *Did he know something I didn't? Did he somehow know?* I thought irrationally, feeling panic prickle against my skin.

"I think it's great you're out enjoying college and letting loose. I don't think you need to feel guilty about having some fun in the middle of what's been going on with Charlie. We're best friends, Clo. I'm going to be there for you, but maybe we don't have to tell each other every single thing that happens to us?" He then chuckled, but it sounded forced and out of place. "Meeting new people and sleeping around happens. Maybe we don't need to share every graphic detail about our conquests?"

"But…" I wanted to explain to him that wasn't why I was telling him about what had happened the previous night.

"Clo, We're both single, and sleeping around is just a part of the whole college experience. Casual sex is not a big deal. These are our experimental years. These are the years we're supposed to make those silly mistakes and grow from them. I've had my fair share of fun, but I doubt you want me to go into the details of those escapades. So maybe we can spare each other the possible awkwardness, and agree to just not get into the details of our sex lives?"

"Oh. Okay. That's fine." I wasn't sure why, but his words stung. Was it because he didn't give me a chance to let him hear what I had to say? Was it because he was okay with me sleeping around, and maybe even encouraging it? Or was it because he just told me he was having his fair share of casual sex?

I didn't know what it was, but his words rubbed me the wrong way. So after a few more minutes of catching up and talking about what classes we were taking, I lied and said I was tired and had an early morning class and needed to get ready for bed.

It was only 8:30, and I wasn't at all tired. But after I got off the phone, I lay in bed in silence thinking about what he'd said, and at some point I fell asleep.

***

I wasn't sure how long I had been out, but my phone suddenly rang, waking me up. I grabbed the phone, thinking it might be Jackson again.

But it wasn't. I frowned at a number I didn't recognize, but decided to answer in case it might have been the hospital where Charlie was staying.

"Hello?"

"Miss Chloe," came an unfamiliar voice on the other line. "My name is Madam Celine and I just received a call from an extremely happy client. He gave me your information and asked if he could book another appointment with you."

"He did?" I was flabbergasted. Part of me felt flattered, part of me felt insulted, and all of me felt oddly excited.

"I would like to extend an invitation to be a part of my escort agency. If you decide to accept the invitation, I am prepared to offer you premium perks."

My instinct was to hang up and throw away Michael's number, but then my eyes landed on the marks on the wall next to my bed that showed the progress of how tall Charlie had grown as a child, and I hesitated. I knew right then that Aunt Betty and Uncle Tom couldn't lose this house; there were too many memories here. It was too important. Despite what Jackson said, if they lost this house, it would be all because of me. It would be my fault.

I knew I had to find a way to help them keep this house and maybe this was it. I listened to her offer and when she was done, all I could see was how much money this would all mean, and how much easier everything would be for Aunt Betty and Uncle Tom if we had all that money. Still, I told her I needed time to think about it.

"You have twenty-four hours to consider my offer and then we'll need to arrange a different escort to accompany Mr. Davison," Madam Celine said matter-of-factly and then the line went dead.

I lay awake half the night, tossing and turning as I tried to decide what to do. It had made me feel so cheap and dirty when I found that money on the nightstand and discovered Michael had thought I was an escort. Still, I had felt ashamed of myself since I ruined the lives of the amazing people who loved and raised me, so what was a little more self-loathing?

The only thing that might make me feel better was to right the wrong I had committed and pay off their hospital bills. Making three grand in one night sure was a quick way to do that, and it wasn't all bad. I didn't want to admit to it, but it had been sort of fun pretending to be someone else—someone who didn't have any problems or guilt, someone who was sexy, powerful, and uninhibited. Plus, after a few drinks, it had been easy to enjoy the uncomplicated, no-strings-attached sex and make Michael think I'd wanted him as much as he'd wanted me.

The one thing I knew for sure was if I decided to accept this offer, no one could know. I couldn't tell Aunt Betty or Uncle Tom. I couldn't tell anyone at school. And most importantly, I couldn't tell Jackson. I cringed at the thought of what he'd think of me if he found out. He'd grown up with money. Would he even understand how I felt right at that moment? Would he even understand how much I was willing to give up and sacrifice to make sure Aunt Betty and Uncle Tom didn't sell the house? I wasn't sure he would. I was sure that he would never look at me the same way again. I was sure that he would break his promise to marry me.

But the thought of possibly losing Jackson if I accepted the offer made my heart ache so much that I felt a need to tell him everything. It was at that moment when I needed my best friend more than ever. *Maybe I should tell him about what happened the other night and about Aunt Betty and Uncle Tom's money problems. Maybe I should tell him everything. Would he understand that I need to take this offer?* I looked over at the alarm clock on my bedside table. It was three in the morning. He was probably already asleep. *I'll call him first thing in the morning.*

***

As soon as my eyes opened the next day, I picked up my phone and called Jackson.

To my surprise, he didn't answer his phone. A woman did.

"Is Jackson there?" I asked, wondering if I dialed the wrong number.

"Yeah, Jackson's here. He's just getting out of the shower." She giggled. "Hold on." I could hear lots of rustling in the background.

"Hello?" came Jackson's voice on the line.

"Hey, Jax. It's me."

"Hey, Clo." I heard him draw in a sharp intake of breath. "I'm kind of busy right now. Can I call you back later?" He sounded out of breath and I wondered if I had interrupted more than just a shower.

"I'm not sure I can wait for another no-call from you," I retorted. "This will just take a minute." I was surprised by my own words, but I wasn't letting him hang up on me again and then never call me back. With only twenty-four hours to decide what to do, I needed to talk to him about this now. I needed my best friend.

"Okay, but make it fast," he urged under his breath. "I have a friend over."

His comment stung a bit, but I decided to brush it off. Now came the hard part. I hadn't actually thought about what I'd say to him, or how I'd bring it up. But now there was no more time to think through that anymore.

Taking a deep breath for courage, I asked, "So the guy I got drunk with and slept with the other night? I'd never met him before, and I don't have feelings for him. But it all happened so fast, and—"

"Clo, I'm sorry, but I really can't talk right now. And like I said last night, sleeping around is just a part of the whole college experience. It's not a big deal. Don't be so serious all the time, Clo. You don't need to be telling me about every guy you sleep with, and to be honest, I really don't want to know."

"But…"

"Look, I don't want to sound like an ass, but in high school, we never really talked to each other about the people we dated. You'd never seemed to like it when I talked about the girls I hooked up with, so I stopped telling you. And now, I kind of feel the same way. I don't really need to hear about the guys you're hooking up with. It doesn't mean we're not best friends or I don't care about you any less."

"So you're saying you're okay with and won't judge me for sleeping around with guys who I have no feelings for?" I asked with an edge of annoyance, feeling hurt by the matter-of-fact tone of his words to me.

"No, of course I won't judge you. There's nothing wrong with having some fun in college. You worry too much, Clo; you always have. From what you told me last night, I think you going out and having some fun and letting loose a bit will be good for you. Don't be so stressed out all the time."

I thought back to the last few times I'd tried to call him and realized that he was definitely having plenty of fun in college. So why did I feel so bad after sleeping with that guy? I hadn't known that he thought I was an escort. And why would that even really matter? It was clear that Jackson was sleeping around with girls—that Tyler guy said he was having a threesome with two girls the other night. If he could have no-strings-attached sex, why couldn't I? Jackson had made it clear that we were both single and didn't need to answer to anyone. So why did I feel the need to get Jackson's approval? Had he ever asked for mine?

"Clo? Are you still there?" Jackson's voice broke through my thoughts, suddenly sounding concerned for the first time since we'd been talking on the phone. *That's just too little and too late.*

"Yeah, Jax. I'm still here. I've been wrestling with a big decision, but I think you've just made it a lot easier for me. So thanks for that. I hope you have a good rest of the day with your *friend*."

"Is everything okay? Do you want me to come out there and we can talk?"

I was so confused by him and how he could switch so quickly from being an asshole to being my best friend. But I realized that it was too late. There was nothing he could say that would change my mind. He'd made it clear that college was a time for having fun, making mistakes, and experimenting. If he were to turn around and tell me we shouldn't be sleeping around in college after he found out what I'd really called him about, I'd know that he was just lying to me.

"No, Jax, you've told me everything I needed to hear. You don't need to come down to see me. I'm fine. Go back to your girls and your fun. I'll talk to you later."

Before he had a chance to respond, I hung up on him. I felt a strange rush of confidence and conviction. I quickly pulled up another number before I could change my mind.

"Hello?"

"Madam Celine?"

"Yes, speaking."

"It's Chloe."

"Ahhh, Ms. Chloe. So have you decided?"

For a moment, I hesitated. Am I making the right decision here? As if to answer my question, I heard Jackson's words ring in my head: "…sleeping around is just a part of the whole college experience.

It's not a big deal. Don't be so serious all the time, Clo." I thought back to the sheer tears of relief in Aunt Betty's eyes when I gave her the envelope full of money the day before, and I knew my answer.

"Yes. I'll take the job," I said boldly.

"That's exactly what I wanted to hear, love." Her voice was as sweet and smooth as honey when she was happy. For the next half an hour, she went over everything I needed to know about being an escort—everything except how to live with the shame. When the conversation was over, I felt overwhelmed and numb as I walked into my bathroom and turned on the shower. As the hot water hit my naked body, I slumped down onto the floor, sat under the unyielding downpour of water, and sobbed.

But even through the tears and fear, I was clear about one thing.

There was no turning back now. At this point, what Jackson or anyone else thought of me, or would think of me, wasn't the most important thing to me.

That wasn't my priority anymore. My priority now was to do everything in my power to make sure my selfishness on my birthday didn't ruin the lives of those I loved more than it already had. I was going to make sure Aunt Betty and Uncle Tom didn't lose their house if it was the last thing I was going to do.

Chapter Thirteen

December 2003

Nineteen Years Old

Jackson

We were lying side by side in a meadow of tall grass and yellow wildflowers under a cloudless sky of perfect blue. I knew immediately where we were. It was one of our favorite spots to go together—the park with the small lake.

It was the place where we'd sealed our pact to marry each other with the love-lock.

"I love you, Chloe. I always have," I whispered to her as I stroked her face with my hand. My throat felt tight and dry with anticipation as I held my breath waiting for her response. If she didn't say it back to me, I knew the pain would be more than I could bear.

She wrapped her arms around my neck and pulled me toward her. She beamed at me before kissing me with her sweet, soft lips. They tasted like honey and felt as soft as the petals of a delicate flower. As she gazed into my eyes, she whispered back, "I love you, too, Jax. I've just been waiting for you to say it."

I felt my chest explode with happiness, and I wondered if she could hear how loud my heart was beating for her.

Then to my surprise, she unzipped her sweater and revealed her naked breasts to me. They were the most beautiful things I'd ever seen.

"Make love to me, Jax" she begged and I saw the need in her eyes. It was the same need that I'd carried inside me for so *long. I wasted no time and bent my head forward to taste her breast in my mouth for the first time.*

I was suddenly ripped from my dream by the blaring sounds of my alarm clock going off.

"Shut that damn thing off, baby," the no-name brunette lying next to me groaned. She rolled over on top of me, squishing her enormous tits against my face as she pressed the button to silence the alarm. They practically smothered me, and I had to open my mouth, gasping for breath.

"Mmm, baby. That feels good. I love the way your mouth feels on me. Want to have a quickie before class?"

My cock was rock hard from my dream about Chloe, but it didn't feel right to have sex with another girl when the one girl I really wanted to be inside of was Chloe. Peeling myself from her arms, I said, "Not right now. Professor Bielman is handing out the take-home final at the beginning of today's econ lecture. I can't be late."

I retreated to the shower, locking the door so she couldn't follow me in. I don't know why I'd called her late last night. It was the first night I'd had to myself in a while, and the first time the frat house wasn't having something going on. So I was sober and ready to call it a night. I even got a chance to catch up with Chloe. I felt like shit hearing what she had been going through and I hated myself for not being able to make time for her the previous times she'd called and texted. I was going to tell her that I wanted to visit her that weekend before finals started. With my parents' divorce, I was heading to my grandparents' house in Vermont with my mom and spending the winter break there, so I wasn't going to see her at all. But when I was about to suggest a visit, she brought up her drunk night with some guy. I never thought she was the type to get drunk and sleep around. But maybe she was having just as much fun in college as I was. So when I'd gotten off the phone with Chloe, I'd remembered the cute brunette that'd given me her number the night before, and I ended up giving her a call.

There was a point during the call when I had an urge to tell Chloe how I felt, to tell her I loved her. But I held back, just like all the other times I had. I wanted her to know, but when it came down to telling her, I just couldn't bring myself to do it. What if she didn't say she loved me back? Or worse, what if she said she loved me but just as a friend. I wasn't sure I could take that amount of rejection. Plus, once she knew how I felt, it would put a huge strain on our friendship if she didn't feel the same way. Eventually, the awkwardness might drive her away from me and then I wouldn't even have her as a friend. That wasn't worth the risk. It was better to keep things the way they were. At least this way we would still be best friends, and I'd still have her in my life. Then there was always our pact. When we both turned thirty, she promised she would marry me. I couldn't imagine loving anyone else. I knew I could hold out until I was thirty. I just hoped that she would, too.

Chapter Fourteen

Spring 2005

Twenty Years Old

Chloe

"It was so good seeing you this week, Charlie." I beamed down at him as I wheeled him down the driveway to where my car was.

"You too, kiddo! I can't believe you have to work during spring break."

I gave him a small smile. "I don't mind. I wasn't planning on going anywhere for spring break."

"Oh? What's Jackson doing?"

"His spring break was last week, and he did that whole Cancun-spring-break-trip thing with his fraternity brothers."

He raised an eyebrow at me. "How come you aren't going on some crazy spring break this week?"

"Work, remember?" I gave a whatever-shrug.

"You should have ditched school the week before and gone with Jackson to spring break," he teased. "You shouldn't be missing out on all the fun just for work."

"A girl tagging along with a bunch of frat guys on a spring break trip to Cancun." I laughed. "I don't think so. I'm pretty sure they're going to be doing plenty of things on this trip they don't want a girl to witness."

"You're probably right." Charlie laughed. "Ahh, to be young and irresponsible again."

"Yeah." I knew I didn't have the normal college experience like Jackson was having. I couldn't remember the last time I actually felt young and irresponsible.

"So what's up with you and Jackson anyway?" He looked at me and I saw a vague hint of concern in his eyes.

"What do you mean?"

"Are you guys still good friends?"

"Yeah, we are. We've hit a rough patch our freshman year because we weren't really on the same page with how to be best friends when going to different schools, but I think since then, we've gotten the hang of it. We try to catch up every couple of weeks, but it's definitely harder to be in each other's day-to-day lives."

He nodded with understanding. "Yeah, long distance does make everything harder."

I frowned, wondering if he was talking about himself. Uncle Tom mentioned that his law firm in Chicago had let him go because they couldn't create a work-from-home position for him.

"Anyway, I'd better get back inside and help Mom with putting the dishes in the dishwasher."

"Okay. It was so good to see you, Charlie." I knelt over and swung my arms around him to give him a big hug.

"You too, Chloe. So when am I going to see my favorite cousin next?"

"Maybe in two weeks? And for the record, I'm your *only* cousin, but I'll take that as a compliment." I scrunched my nose at him.

"Correction," he didn't waste a second countering me, "you're my only *immediate* cousin. But I should warn you, I have a number of distant cousins you're competing against for that top spot. So don't get too comfortable at number one."

I giggled. "Damn, does that mean I need to continue to be nice to you next time I see you?" I teased back.

"Wait, you've been nice to me?" His words came out in an exaggerated tone of surprise.

"Ha, very funny," I replied sarcastically. "Well, I'll see you soon. And I hope you've been doing well at home."

He shrugged cheerfully. "Not bad. Life's pretty easy when you're on an extended vacation."

I smiled down at him, but on the inside I felt the guilt, which now permanently lived inside—twist in the pit of my stomach. It'd been over a year since the accident, and Charlie had been released from the hospital five months earlier. Since then, he'd been continuing his extensive physical therapy as he adjusted to life in a wheelchair and living with Aunt Betty and Uncle Tom.

There was a period right after the accident where Charlie hadn't been his happy-go-lucky self. During that time, he had fallen into a deep state of depression. He hadn't wanted to see anyone or be taken anywhere. It'd killed Aunt Betty and Uncle Tom to see him in such a state, which only intensified the all-consuming guilt that I'd tried to live with.

But at some point, he'd somehow accepted his fate and the always-cheerful and optimistic Charlie I'd grown up with had returned. He acted like nothing bad had ever happened to him. While I was happy to see Charlie happy again, seeing his ability to make the best of everything only reminded me of the part I played in his fate, and this only fueled my determination to continue my secret job as an escort.

After I waved goodbye to Charlie and reversed my car out of the driveway, I looked down at my watch to check the time. I had to work in the city tonight and it was a new client, so I didn't want to be late.

It'd been almost a year since I'd officially become an escort for Madam Celine. While I didn't love what I did and would always need a hot shower after a client had left, each time became easier than the last to compartmentalize what I was doing with these men. What was most important, and what I'd always reminded myself, was that I was able to pay for Charlie's medical bills without Aunt Betty and Uncle Tom needing to sell the house. And it was the relief I'd see on their faces, when they'd get their monthly payments in the mail, that kept me going.

As I pulled up to the valet line in front of the Four Seasons hotel in downtown Philadelphia, the valet came around to my side of the car to open the door for me. I gave him my keys and grabbed my tote from the backseat that contained my change of clothes and makeup. I quickly went to the restroom in the lobby to get ready before heading up the elevator to the hotel room listed on the instructions Madam Celine had emailed me.

When I got to Room 509, I noticed the door was propped open by the bar latch. My instructions told me that this new client liked to incorporate mystery into his fantasy and I had to make sure to play along.

"Hello?" I called out in a soft, seductive voice, as I gently pushed through the door and walked inside. I found the room dimly lit with soft jazz playing in the background. The room appeared to be empty. My eyes spotted a white notecard and a black silk blindfold on the console in the entryway. I walked over to it and read the note:

Chloe,

I want you to feel everything I do to you tonight. Put on this blindfold and wait for me in the bed. When you're ready, just tell me how wet you are for me and I'll come out of the bathroom.

- Ian

My eyes darted over to the closed bathroom door and realized my client was already here.

As I felt the three shots of vodka I'd had a few minutes before in the restroom work their way into my system, loosening my inhibition and arousing my senses, I sucked in a deep breath and mentally prepared myself.

Just like Jax said. We're both single. Sleeping around is just a part of the whole college experience. Casual sex is not a big deal. Don't be so serious all the time, Clo.

I repeated Jax's word to myself. Over the last year, it'd become something of a mantra that I'd chant before I'd meet my clients.

Letting out another deep breath, I took the blindfold from the console and walked over to the bed. I positioned my body provocatively before putting the blindfold on. As I felt the cool silk brush against my face and blind me completely, I couldn't help but feel a little vulnerable and scared. But I quickly pushed the thought from my mind and tried to get into character. *This may not be something the normal Chloe would do, but the sexy, adventurous, and uninhibited Chloe likes a little mystery and casual fun, and she is going to enjoy herself tonight.*

"Hey, baby. Come on out and feel for yourself how ready I am for you," I purred in my sexiest voice.

I heard him walk into the room, and by his sudden inhale of breath, I knew he liked what he saw.

"Damn, you're more beautiful than I had imagined."

I gasped in surprised when I felt his rough hands move across my body like he owned me.

"What do you want to do to me tonight?" I asked, trying to stay in character.

"Tonight, baby, I'm going to show you how a real man fucks a beauty like you. Now, tell me you want to be fucked by a real man."

Something about his voice put me on edge, and I suddenly felt uneasy. But I quickly brushed it aside as I willed the vodka to work faster through my system.

"I want to be fucked by a real man like you, baby." I flashed Ian a smile, motioning him to get closer to me. "Now show me what you got."

He didn't need to be asked twice, because a second later, I felt the sensation of his hot, wet mouth on my bare neck, throat, and shoulders. He kissed his way down my chest, slowly peeling away the layers of my dress until my breasts were exposed. I gasped in surprise and pleasure as he took my full breasts into his firm hands and roughly fondled them.

Then I felt his hungry mouth engulf my breasts and suck my nipples, one at a time, flicking them eagerly with his tongue as he groaned in pleasure.

I threw back my head and arched my back, inviting him to explore me further.

"Fuck, you taste amazing," he said through ragged breaths and I knew he was close to losing control.

"Baby, you're making me so wet," I purred. I reached for his hand and pulled it down my inner thighs and guided his fingers along the wet fabric of my panties.

"You're so wet for me, you're driving me so crazy, I can't wait another second to be inside you."

"Give it to me, Ian. Show me how a real man fucks," I encouraged.

"Once I fuck you, Chloe, you'll never forget it." He groaned as I heard him rip open a condom.

I moaned in response and squirmed my body to show him my anticipation.

I cried out suddenly as he pulled down my panties and spread my legs wide apart with one swift movement.

"Tell me how much you want this," he demanded as I felt the tip of his erection move up and down my wetness between my thighs.

"I want to feel you deep inside me," I panted.

I heard him groan in pleasure as he plunged himself all the way inside of me in one fast thrust.

"Fuck, you're so hard and big, baby!" I cried out as I rocked my hips in time with his thrusts.

He drove himself inside of me in rapid succession, and to my surprise, he didn't last long. In just under a minute, he'd reached his climax as he plunged into me one last time before he spasmed uncontrollably and reached his release.

Seconds later, I heard him fall back onto the bed next to me with a satisfied grunt.

I let out an obligatory sign of satisfaction. "Baby, that was amazing."

He chuckled. "I can't believe how tight your pussy is. I wanted to go for longer, but you drove me crazy and I just completely lost it."

I smiled. "I'm here to make you happy, Ian."

"Now, take off your blindfold, Chloe. That'll make me happy."

His demand sounded abrupt, but I didn't think anything of it. I obeyed and removed the blindfold off my face.

I turned to flash Ian a sexy smile, but when I met his eyes, I gasped and leaped away from him.

"It can't be!" I gasped, suddenly feeling queasy.

The man who was smiling back at me, the man who had just been inside me, the man who was my new client was *John Pierce*. Jackson's father.

He smiled widely at me as he got up and approached me. "Don't play coy with me, Chloe. You knew it was me."

"No!" I shook my head violently, both in disagreement with his statement and in utter disbelief that it was him who was standing in front of me at that moment. "I didn't know it was you! How can you even say that?" I quickly put on my clothes, feeling sick to my stomach.

"But we've been so close for all these years, you must know the sound of my voice by now." He had an almost evil grin on his face, and I wasn't sure if he was taunting me or actually delusional.

"Mr. Pierce, we can't be doing this." I shook my head violently, wishing that the prior fifteen minutes hadn't happened.

"Chloe, what did I tell you about calling me, Mr. Pierce. It's *John* to you," he laughed, "or Ian—it's my middle name, after all. But with how close we've become, especially in the last half hour, I don't think Mr. Pierce sounds right at all."

Suddenly I felt my stomach churn and I ran as fast as I could to the bathroom. I locked the door behind me before turning around and throwing up into the toilet, feeling more sick with each passing minute.

Tears flowed down my face and clouded my vision as I sobbed, trying to figure out how this had happened—*why* this had happened.

Then a knock came at the door. "Chloe, let's talk about this. Let me in," Mr. Pierce said from the other side of the door.

"We can talk just fine with the door between us," I managed to retort.

"Come on, don't be like this. I'm not sure why you're so upset. We're not doing anything wrong here."

We're not doing anything wrong here? I screamed inside. "You're Jackson's dad! What happened wasn't right, it's forbidden."

I heard him laugh. "Forbidden? Forbidden by whom? We're two single, consenting adults having a good time. And before you took off that blindfold, I don't think I was the only one having a good time. Now what's wrong with that?"

"But you're Jackson's dad…he's…he's my best friend." I felt my body go numb with shock.

"So? Who cares if I'm Jackson's dad? This has nothing to do with him."

"But this has *everything* to do with him!" I heard myself scream at the door.

"Why? Is Jackson your boyfriend and I didn't get the memo?" There was a mocking tone to his voice, which hurt and angered me at the same time.

"No, but…"

"Well there you go, then. You and Jackson are just friends. From what Madam Celine tells me, you're single. So explain to me what's so wrong about that?"

I opened my mouth, but then closed it. I wasn't sure what to say, because I didn't have a clear answer. Even though it wasn't technically wrong, in the legal sense, it felt very wrong to be having sex with Mr. Pierce.

"Ask yourself this: if Jackson were a girl, and you were best friends with my daughter, would you still think our interaction would be forbidden or wrong?"

"I..." I didn't know what to say. There was some truth in what he'd just asked. There was something that felt wrong with what'd just happened because Jackson was a guy, and maybe I wouldn't feel as strongly about it if Jackson were a girl. But as hard as I tried, I couldn't wrap my mind around why it would be different.

"Do you like Jackson or something?"

His question made me feel uneasy. *Like Jackson? Like my best friend?* That was something I'd never thought about before.

"Well, I should tell you now that you should stop wasting your time. Jackson sees you as his sister and friend, nothing else."

The thought that Jackson thought of me like a sister made me more upset than I could understand.

Then another question came to me. "How did you arrange this? How did you find me? And why? Why me?" My questions rushed out in rapid succession as my brain tried to process how all this had happened. *How can life be this twisted?*

"Well, I discovered Madam Celine and her *services* recently. Since my divorce, I'd gotten really lonely, and quite frankly, horny. So I was going through her portfolio of girls, and I couldn't believe my eyes when I landed on the page with your pictures." He let out a loud sigh of pleasure, and I could tell he was leaning into the door between us while he spoke.

"But why me?" I repeated. "There are so many other options, girls much more popular with Madam Celine's clients than I am. Why did you have to pick me? You've known me since I was a kid. Wouldn't that make me the last option you'd pick in her portfolio of girls?"

"Chloe, now that's a silly question. You must know that I've had my eyes on you since you were sixteen. My son's an idiot for not making a move on you. I've tried to show you how I feel about you, but you were just too innocent to even know. You have no idea how much that innocence drove me over the edge. I was really disappointed when you never came to see me when you started at Penn. I guess you didn't get my hints. So you'd better believe I was pleasantly surprised when I was looking for a long term no-strings-attached lady friend through Madam Celine and came across your photos. Damn, Chloe, I must say, those are some amazing photos Madam Celine has got in that portfolio of you, but nothing compares to seeing you in the flesh, and feeling you respond to my touch and my body."

I felt sick hearing his words, and all the past memories of his odd behaviors when we were alone began to flood back to me and take on a new light and meaning. I hugged my bent knees tightly as I rocked back and forth on the bathroom floor, trying to somehow will tonight from existence.

"Why did you blindfold me? Why did you make me have sex with you without knowing it was you?"

"Because I wanted to show you that you'd have fun with me if you didn't let your feelings for Jackson get in the way and cloud your judgment. If he was really interested in you, he would have made his move a long time ago. So if you're single, and spreading that tight pussy for random men you don't know, why not spread it for me?"

At that point, I couldn't take it anymore. I wanted—and needed— to get out of there. I just couldn't listen to what he had to say one second longer. I got up, took in a deep breath to calm my nerves, and opened the door.

His eyes lit up as soon as he saw me, but I didn't give him a chance to get a word in.

"Don't fucking touch me!" With all the force I could muster, I pushed him back with both of my hands. As he stumbled backward, I ran past him and out of Room 509 as fast as I could, not daring to look back.

***

When the valet arrived with my car, I quickly paid and got in before speeding off. It wasn't until I was several miles out from the hotel that I'd finally slowed down.

I pulled over to the side of the street and tried to calm myself. This couldn't happen again. I reached for my phone and dialed Madam Celine's number.

"Hello?"

"Madam Celine, this is Chloe Sinclair. I know it might be a little late to call," I said, looking at my watch and seeing that it said 10:20, "but this is an emergency."

"What is it, Chloe? Aren't you supposed to be with a new client right now?" I could hear the worry in her voice.

"I'm calling about that, actually."

"What is it? Did you meet him? Is everything okay?"

"Yes, I met him, but everything's not okay. I know this client through my personal life."

"Okay?"

"He's my best friend's father. I've known him since I was seven."

"And?" It was clear she didn't see a problem with that. "Did he complain? Did he not know it was you?"

"No, that's just it. He knew it was me when he signed up. But I can't see him again."

"Is that what he wants?"

"I don't know. Does it matter? I'm telling you *I* can't do it. He can't be a repeat client for me."

"Chloe, unless there's some legal issue, or something I can use to tell the client that he can't have what he wants—and has already had—I'm afraid that's not a request I can agree with. This is a new client, but with his connections in the area, I see him as a client I want to keep happy for both his repeat business and his referral business. Plus, like my motto says, 'Client comes first.'"

I wanted to say her motto was "Clients *cum* first," but I didn't think arguing over that would help my cause. But I didn't back down from the issue. Instead, I pushed further. "What if I refused to see him again? Could he just be reassigned to someone else?"

"Chloe, let me make this clear to you one last time," the growing impatience clear in her voice, "Who your client is, it's *not* your choice, it's not even my choice. It's the client's. So if the client still wants to see you, then you'll see him, and you'll see him with a smile on your face and your thighs wide open for his pleasure."

I swallowed. "So there's nothing I can do to change that?"

"No, you can't pick and choose who you are with. If this client wants to see you again, and you refuse, then I'll have to terminate our agreement and your position at the agency. Do I need to remind you of our contract?"

"No, you don't. I think you've made it perfectly clear what my options are."

My arrangement with Madam Celine was a unique one, and before I had agreed to be one of her girls about a year ago, we'd drafted up a contract that set out a number of terms.

First, she agreed to my request to keep my number of clients low and "dates" less frequent compared to her other girls. I had school and had joined a few social groups on campus during my spring semester freshman year. I only wanted to make enough every month to pay for the monthly medical installment payments and the bills Aunt Betty and Uncle Tom were receiving.

Second—and the unique portion of our agreement—I'd agree to work for her for a period of two years, and in exchange for a total of $500,000.00, after taxes, to be paid in monthly installments, and paid directly to Aunt Betty and Uncle Tom. That was the total amount of medical bills Aunt Betty and Uncle Tom needed to pay off. Under the contract, Madam Celine had reached out to Aunt Betty and Uncle Tom last year to inform them that they were the grand prize winners of a raffle they'd entered at the mall the year before. Although neither Aunt Betty nor Uncle Tom could recall entering any raffles, as predicted, they didn't question anything and were more than happy to accept the monthly installment payments for a period of two years. Under the contract, if I stopped being an escort before the two-year period ended, the monthly payments would stop immediately.

This second term in my agreement with Madam Celine had been something I'd insisted on. It was the only way I could think of to ensure that Aunt Betty and Uncle Tom would accept such a large sum of money without questioning its source. It was one thing for Aunt Betty to believe I had three grand in my savings, but quite another thing for her to believe I was able to get my hands on half a million dollars.

There had been another reason why I didn't want Aunt Betty and Uncle Tom to know that I was the source of the money. I didn't deserve to be treated like I was some hero who came and saved them from their financial crisis when I was the whole reason why they were in the crisis to begin with.

By the time I hung up the phone with Madam Celine, I knew that if I wanted Aunt Betty and Uncle Tom to continue to receive their monthly payments, I had to continue to see Mr. Pierce if he requested me. If I refused to see him, Madam Celine would terminate our contract and I'd no longer be an escort for her agency, and Aunt Betty and Uncle Tom would stop receiving the money, and they'd probably lose the house.

I was at a loss and had no idea what to do. There was still a year left on my contract with Madam Celine, and about a quarter of a million dollars left in unpaid medical bills. I knew there was no way I could get my hands on that much money in a year's time.

But this is Jackson's dad? How can I even consider continuing down this path? I can't do that to Jackson!

I felt torn between my obligation toward Aunt Betty, Uncle Tom, and Charlie, and Jackson. How could I possible choose between the two options?

I didn't know what I was going to do, but I did know one thing: I had to see Jackson right away and tell him what happened.

***

My eyes felt dry and heavy as I gulped down the rest of my morning coffee. It was almost ten in the morning the next day and I was only a few minutes from Jackson's fraternity house. Unable to fall asleep after the previous night's events, I'd left Philadelphia just before five in the morning. During the entire five-hour drive, I replayed over and over again everything that'd happened the night before.

I knew that I needed to talk to Jackson. He'd told me before that he didn't want to hear about the guys I'd slept with, but I think this had to be an exception. He might not want to know, but sleeping with his father was not something I wanted to keep from him.

When I pulled up in front of the frat house, I saw a few guys mulling around in the yard, cleaning up the beer cans and red SOLO cups obviously left over from last night's party. *Must be pledges*, I thought to myself.

I checked my phone to see if Jackson's responded to my text messages telling him I was coming into town. Nothing.

The front door of the frat house had already been propped open, so I decided to check to see if he was already awake. I knew I was being crazy for going there unannounced, but after what had happened the night before, I just needed to tell Jackson as soon as possible.

Except for a couple of guys and girls passed out on the various couches in the common area, the first floor of the house was empty. I headed up to Jackson's room, remembering it from the handful of times I'd visited him within the last year that he'd lived here.

When got to Jackson's door, I thought I heard him talking inside. But when I knocked, no one answered. *Maybe he didn't hear me.* Without another thought, I opened the door and walked in.

I gasped at what I saw. But my gasps were drowned out by the even-louder cries of the naked girl with long, strawberry blonde curls cascading down her back. She was straddled on top of Jackson and riding him like there was no tomorrow. Jackson's hands gripped her waist as he thrust up in time with her hips.

I tried to back out of the room before they saw me standing there, but it was too late.

"Fuck! Chloe? What the fuck are you doing here?" Jackson screamed when he spotted me, and I watched as he pushed the blonde off of him.

For a brief moment, I averted my eyes away from Jackson's hard, rigid chest and enormous, throbbing erection, feeling my cheeks flush at the sight of him as my body reacted in a way that I'd never felt before. *Why am I turned on all of a sudden when I see him naked? He's my best friend!*

But when I turned back to face them, my eyes locked onto the last person I was expecting to see, and my body stiffened at the sight of her.

"Don't you know how to knock, Chloe? Or do they not teach you guys that at Penn?" Amber flashed me a condescending smirk as she placed her hands on her perfectly-curved hips.

Amber and Jackson? Shock paralyzed me as I looked between the two of them, unable to believe my eyes.

"Clo, what are you doing here?" Jackson demanded as he put on his boxers.

Unable to speak for fear I'd lose it completely, I bit my lower lip hard, trying as hard as I could to hold back the tears. Feelings of betrayal, rejection, and disappointment crashed through me all at once. I met Jackson's gaze and the look of guilt that twisted in his face only hurt me more. But I refused to let them see how upset I was at that very moment. Before I would allow any tears to fall down my cheeks, I turned from them and fled from the room, leaving behind my best friend and my childhood nemesis.

As I ran down the staircase toward the front door of the frat house, the unrelenting images of their naked bodies grinding against one another flooded through my mind. *You're not together! You're both single! It's just a stupid childhood pact!*

Chapter Fifteen

Spring 2005

Twenty Years Old

Jackson

I was seconds away from reaching my climax when I saw Chloe at the doorway staring at us in shock.

"Fuck! Chloe? What the fuck are you doing here?" I pushed Amber off of me, realizing how bad this must have looked to Chloe.

I saw Chloe's expression change from shock to confusion to pain when she saw that the girl was Amber.

I wanted to say something, but Amber beat me to it.

"Don't you know how to knock, Chloe? Or do they not teach you guys that at Penn?"

At that moment, I wanted to smack Amber across the face for what she'd just said to my best friend. *Has she always talked to Chloe that way? Does she think I somehow favor her over Chloe just because she is one of my fuck buddies?* I wanted to cuss Amber out, but one look at Chloe and I knew that had to wait.

"Clo, what are you doing here?" I grabbed my boxers and slipped them on quickly, feeling unusually self-conscious about her seeing me naked. *Did she like what she saw? Could I possibly turn her on?*

I watched Chloe expectantly, waiting for her to say something. But she just stared at me in silence, biting her lower lip like she was holding herself back from saying anything to me. The pain and disappointment that filled her misty eyes caused my chest to tighten with guilt and shame.

Before I could say another word, she suddenly turned around and ran out of my room. I leaped to my feet, ready to go after her. But Amber stepped in front of me, pressing her palm against my chest to stop me.

"We should let her go. She shouldn't have barged in on us like that. There's nothing we can say to her to make her feel better."

"What the fuck are you talking about, Amber?" I spat out as I knocked her hand off my chest. "There is no 'we' between us, and I wouldn't hold my breath waiting for this to ever turn into a 'we' situation."

Amber recoiled at my words and I saw the indignation on her face, shocked that anyone would treat her that way. I realized then that I'd never snapped at her before. I'd always thought she'd grown up and wasn't the self-absorbed "mean girl" like she had been in elementary school. But when I saw how she'd treated Chloe moments ago, I realized that Chloe was right. Amber hadn't changed for the better—if anything, she was worse than she was in first grade.

Without another word to Amber, I moved around her and ran out the door after Chloe.

By the time I got outside, Chloe was already in her car, about to start her engine.

"Clo!" I called out to stop her as I ran to her car.

She looked over at me and my chest tightened at the sight of tears in her bloodshot eyes.

"This was a bad idea, Jax. I shouldn't have stopped by without confirming with you first."

"No, it's okay. Clo, come out of the car and let's talk. I know you wouldn't drive this far to see me if it wasn't important. What happened?"

But she ignored my question and glared at me. "Why are you sleeping with Amber? How could you do that to me?"

I flinched at her questions and suddenly felt as if I needed to defend myself. "Clo, I know you don't like her, and to be honest, I don't care for her either, but it's just sex."

"But how can you have sex with *her* of all people?"

Her question again left me feeling defensive. I didn't know why, but I felt a strong urge to apologize. But what was I apologizing for? For sleeping with a girl she didn't like, or for something more? *But she's not my girlfriend! I don't owe an apology if I haven't done anything wrong.*

"Look, she just came over for the house party last night and we had a bit too much to drink. It was just sex. It's not a big deal. I'm not somehow favoring her over you. You'll always be my best friend, and she's an acquaintance at best. It's not something you should be upset about and cry over."

I thought she'd relax after I tried to reassure her, but instead, her expression became stone cold. "I know we're just best friends and you see me like your sister and maybe that's why you don't like us talking to each other about our sex lives, but can you honestly tell me that you don't see anything wrong with you sleeping with Amber?"

Her sister? What was she talking about? *Does she only see me as a brother-figure?* I was so thrown off balance by that comment that I realized I hadn't heard the rest of her question.

"What was your question?"

I saw her face twist with annoyance. "I asked, do you honestly think you didn't do anything wrong when you slept with Amber? You know I don't like her. You know how mean she's always been to me."

I sighed, feeling like our conversation was going in circles. "Clo, I'm not trying to be an ass here, but

I'm really not sure why you're so upset. I don't see anything wrong with having casual sex with someone. It has nothing to do with our friendship, and it doesn't affect our friendship at all."

"How do you figure?" she retorted, demanding me to elaborate. "How does that *not* affect our friendship? You just fucked a girl who has it out for me."

Now it was my turn to be annoyed. How could she be so upset with me? It wasn't like we were in a relationship or anything. It wasn't like I was cheating on her. "Because it was *just* sex. Clo, I don't know how many different ways I can say this. It's casual sex and it has nothing to do with our friendship. I'm not any better friends with her than I was before fucking her. I don't care any more about her than I had before fucking her. Our friendship, and my feelings toward you, hasn't changed for me because I've fucked her."

"So let me get this straight. From what you're saying, I can just sleep with anyone I want, even if it's someone you don't want me to sleep with? And I don't need your approval and that it's okay because it's just sex and doesn't mean a thing?"

I wasn't sure what she was trying to get at with her questions, but I could tell she was upset. So I agreed with her without asking further. I was tired of us arguing over something so stupid. "That sounds about right. I can't tell you who you should or shouldn't sleep with. That's your prerogative. And honestly, I don't really want to know."

"You should go back to Amber," she replied flatly as she turned her attention forward and started her engine. "I don't want you to give her the wrong idea about us."

I was confused, and hurt, by her words. If this wasn't her way of telling me she wasn't interested in me, I wasn't sure what was. But I wanted to test her one last time.

"Clo, we're both single. I know you sleep with random guys like I sleep with random girls. Why are you so upset about Amber? Are you jealous?"

I wanted her to say she was, but she didn't. Instead, she locked eyes with me and said coldly, "I came here because I thought I needed to tell you something, because I felt bad and thought it was something that'd affect our friendship. So I wanted to tell you as soon as I could. But after this morning, I think I was wrong about that. You've made it clear that whoever we casually sleep with has no bearing on our friendship. So thanks for saving me the effort of that conversation."

I wanted to ask her what she meant by all that, but before I could, she sped off. I watched her drive off, wondering what all this was about. Had she met someone new that she was interested in? Was she here to tell me about him and how much she liked him—or loved him? Had I somehow just pushed her away and into the arms of that man? My chest ached in pain at the thought and I wondered if my worst fear was being realized: Was Chloe going to fall in love and marry someone before she turned thirty?

Chapter Sixteen

Present Day

Thirty Years Old

Chloe

"Hey, Charlie." I tried to sound cheerful as I walked into the house and saw Charlie at the dining table. My encounter with Jackson was still fresh on my mind and the coldness he had for me continued to grip against my heart, and I found it difficult to breathe when I thought about him. His words today had stung me more than I'd thought possible. And what was worse was that he used to buy me tulips when I was sad, and it seemed ironic that it'd be a bouquet of tulips that was the cause of my current sadness.

"Hey, kiddo. I heard you fainted last night. You okay now?"

I forced a smile. "Yeah, I'm fine. I was just dehydrated. No biggie." I walked over to the table and a genuine smile spread across my face. "Is this the new case you were telling me about the other day?"

Charlie grinned ear to ear as he looked at me. "Yeah. It's a new environmental project the city is doing along the Schuylkill River. There're a lot of possible legal implications from the project, so they're taking me on to help with the research."

"That's so great, Charlie. This is like the sixth project they've sent over to you in the last five years?"

"Yeah, it's been great being able to work again. I can't believe how much I've missed that feeling of contributing to something and being a functioning member of society."

I could tell how happy he was and it almost brought tears to my eyes to know that his life wasn't completely ruined by my selfishness years ago.

"So my mom said you're thinking of moving back to Philly?"

"Yeah." I gave a shrug. "L.A. wasn't what I thought it'd be. So I was going to live with you guys for a bit while I figure things out."

"That's great. I guess you can have your room back." He pretended to be upset.

I giggled. "It was your room first. I don't mind staying in the guest room."

"Nah. I don't want that room. You can have it. After Dad put up all those fake stars on the ceiling, it never felt like a room for a middle-aged guy. So it's all yours, kiddo."

I beamed at him, knowing he was just saying that to let me have the room. "Thanks, Charlie. You're the best."

"Yeah, tell me something I don't know." He gave me a wink before he returned back to his work.

Feeling a little better after talking to Charlie, I decided to take a walk to clear my head and figure out what I was going to do with the rest of my life. When I opened the front door to leave the house, my breath caught in my lungs at who I saw walking up the driveway toward me.

I couldn't believe my eyes. It was Jackson.

He looked up and met my eyes and I stood there, momentarily frozen, wondering what he was doing here. Aunt Betty wasn't coming back home until tomorrow, so he couldn't be here for her. Could he possibly be here to see me? I didn't dare hope for this as a possibility, not after my last few attempts in trying to talk to him. He'd made it perfectly clear to me that he hated me, and there was nothing I could say to change that.

But what was he doing here, then? Deciding to throw caution to the wind at the risk of another heartbreak, I forced my feet to move forward to meet him halfway.

"Hi, Clo," he said softly when we stopped in front of each other.

My heart fluttered when I heard his nickname for me leave his lips. *What does this mean?*

"Hi." The simple word came out breathy from my mouth as I gazed into his eyes, trying to read his thoughts. "What are you doing here?"

"I just got back from the hospital."

"Okay." I felt a trickle of nerves paralyze me as it moved down my body. "Aren't you supposed to be on the train back to New York?"

There was an unusual smile on his face and I couldn't work out what he was thinking.

"I've changed my mind. There is something here that I need to stay for."

"Oh, there is?" I felt disappointed by his words. Had he met a girl last night at the wedding that he was interested in?

"So you know how I said earlier today that I wasn't sure I was ready to talk to you?"

"Yeah."

"Well, I'm ready now…if you're still willing to talk to me."

For a moment, I just stared at him in silence, wondering if I'd heard him correctly.

"Yeah," I responded softly. "I want to talk."

We stood there in silence, expecting the other person to say something first. It then occurred to me that during all this time I'd wanted to talk to Jackson about what happened years ago, I'd never actually thought about what we'd say about when we actually talked.

"Umm. So what do you want to talk about?" I asked, hoping he had something in mind.

"I hadn't actually thought about that yet." I watched him turn and look over his shoulder before he turned back to me and continued, "It's a nice day out. Wanna take a walk?"

I nodded.

We walked in silence for a few minutes. We kept our eyes forward but would occasionally sneak a sideways glance at one another when we didn't think the other person was watching.

Then at the same time he blurted out, "I'm sorry, Clo," I said, "I'm sorry, Jax."

I gave him a small smile. To my surprise, he gave a light chuckle and he flashed me one of his boyish grins.

"Clo, your aunt said some things to me today that made a lot of sense, and it's really got me thinking about what happened to us ten years ago."

"Oh? What did she say?" I felt nerves prickle down my spine again. I hadn't prepared myself for the possibility that Aunt Betty was going to say anything to Jackson.

"She said that I needed to hear your side of the story, that things weren't as simple as I thought they were."

"Yeah, they're not," I agreed softly.

"I'm sorry, Clo. I know that I can be pretty rash and stubborn, and quick to jump to conclusions. After talking to Aunt Betty, I realize that I've never once stopped to listen to your side of the story. That's not what a best friend would do. And thinking back to the two years before that night with my father, I remembered all the times you'd called and texted and I'd ignored you because I was stupid and I was so self-absorbed in my own world to realize something was wrong. I remembered all the times you'd told me point blank that you needed me and I blew you off like your words didn't carry any weight. I really wasn't there for you and I really didn't know what was going on in your life. And yet I turned on you and never gave you a chance to tell me what was going on." He looked away in shame.

Touched by his words, I felt my heart go out to him. "It's okay, Jax. I wasn't always great at being your best friend either. I let my pride dictate a lot of things that had happened, and I wasn't as straight-forward with you as I could have been."

He let out a sigh. "I can't believe it's taken me ten year and a kick in the head by Aunt Betty to finally sit down to hear you out. I'm a total idiot."

"I'm not going to disagree with that." He turned to look at me, and I let out a giggle. Then I shrugged. "It's the truth."

He chuckled and nodded. "Yeah, it is. But I'm here to listen now, Clo. Can you tell me everything that happened during those first few years of college? How did things get so screwed up between us?"

For the next half an hour, I told him about what happened after he didn't show up for my birthday, about how lonely I'd felt, and about how I'd guilt-tripped Aunt Betty, Uncle Tom, and Charlie to visit me. I told him about the accident, about Charlie's medical bills, and about the possibility of losing the house. I told him about being upset with him for not returning my calls or text messages, about going out and having a one-night stand, about how the stranger thought that I was an escort and how I started doing that to secretly pay for Charlie's medical bills. And finally, I told him the most difficult part to tell—I told him about his father, about the times he'd touched me growing up, about how he had me blindfolded our first time so I wouldn't know it was him.

I saw the anguish and anger in Jackson's eyes as I retold that story. I knew it wasn't something anyone wanted to hear about their own father.

"I'm sorry for hurting you, Jax," I said softly. "I never wanted you to find out that way. I'd wanted to tell you everything that had happened, especially with what happened with your dad."

"So why didn't you tell me about what happened with him?" There was a mixture of anger, disappointment, and sorrow in his voice.

"I tried," I assured him. "I wanted to tell you as soon as it happened."

"But how come you never did?"

I paused as all the unpleasant feelings from that moment in time came rushing back to me. "I tried to as soon as I saw that it was your dad. I couldn't sleep that night and I left Philly really early in the morning so that I could get to Harvard around ten in the morning. I figured you'd be up by then."

He frowned. "I don't remember you visiting me to tell me anything."

I cleared my throat. "That was the time I visited you unannounced and I walked in on you having sex with Amber, and then we had that huge fight."

There was a moment of silence, as if he was replaying that moment in his head. Then suddenly, something in his expression changed completely. There was a look of understanding and horror painted across his face. Finally, he turned to look at me, his eyes full of despair, and he murmured in a low, tormented voice, "It's my fault. I told you it was okay. I told you I didn't want to know… I drove you to him."

***

It was almost by instinct, or habit, but as we walked and talked about everything that'd happened in college, we somehow found ourselves in that park with the small lake that was near our houses.

As I snuck a sideways glance at Jackson, I realized that every fond memory of this park included him. The place was less than a mile from our neighborhood and we used to come here for hours at a time. He'd taught me how to skip rocks in the lake—telling me that the trick was to find the flattest rock with the most surface area. I still remember the sheer sense of accomplishment when I'd skipped a rock across the lake and watched it leap five times across the water's surface before it'd disappeared.

"I loved feeding the ducks here when we were younger." Jackson's words interrupted my thoughts, and they caused me to smile. He was also reminiscing on the amazing times we'd had here.

"Me too," I whispered. Our eyes met in a smile, and I saw the familiar warmth in his rich, emerald eyes that I'd yearned for during the past decade.

"Remember the time you fell into the lake and I had to save you?" He laughed at the memories as a wistful expression blanketed his face.

"Umm, no, Jax." I frowned at him "I didn't *fall* into the lake. You *pushed* me into the lake and then tried to play the hero when you rescued me, remember?"

"Really?" He twisted his face as he tried to recall the memory.

"Yes," I said as I shot him an exaggerated glare. "You thought it'd be fun to act out a scene from *The Teenage Mutant Ninja Turtles*. But the only problem was, you forgot to tell me that it was your plan before you pushed me in. You basically just pushed me in and then told me afterward when I was crying." I made a face at him when his face lit up as the memory came back to him.

"Oh yeah. Oops." He chuckled. "Guess boys will be boys." He shrugged and flashed me one of his I'm-so-innocent grins.

I rolled my eyes at him. "That's your excuse for everything."

He laughed and then abruptly stopped as he looked over at me. "I've missed you, Clo." His eyes were full of emotion when I gazed up at him.

Those simple, sincere four words were all that it took for the tears to collect in my eyes.

"I've missed you, too, Jax."

We smiled at each other in silence as we gazed into each other's eyes.

"Hey, let me try something," he said suddenly as he took a step forward, our faces only inches apart. Then he held my gaze without saying another word.

I frowned, feeling a little nervous by the intensity of his stare and the proximity of his body to mine.

But he didn't seem to notice my unease. Instead, his lips curled into a devious grin, and he continued to stare at me, never moving a muscle.

"What?" I finally asked. "What is it?" I giggled nervously. *Is there something disgusting or dirty on my face? Is it a bug?*

"Nothing," was all he said as he flashed me a coy smile.

"Jax, this isn't funny," I warned, feeling uneasy.

Suddenly, he burst into a fit of laughter. "You're pretty adorable when you get nervous, too."

"Too?" I searched his face for an answer, starting to feel annoyed. "What do you mean? Tell me!" I slapped him across the chest, shooting him an evil eye.

He chuckled. "Fine, I'll tell you. Just don't abuse me like that."

I rolled my eyes at his silliness. "I guess some things never change." He was the same boy from decades ago who teased me and called me Pippi Longstocking, the same boy who knew how to push my buttons and annoy the crap out of me.

"No, I'm serious." He gave me a stern look. "Friend-abuse is a really serious problem in this country."

I shook my head, letting him know that I didn't think it was funny.

"Okay, I'll tell you. For reals this time." He grinned and held my gaze. "So a really smart girl who didn't want to be called a nerd once told me that people who love each other can sync up their heart rates by staring into each other's eyes." He then shrugged. "I just wanted to test the theory out."

"You still remember," I gasped as my chest was filled with an indescribable sense of happiness at that moment.

He nodded and looked at me. "Before I was that asshole you'd met during our college years, I think I was a nice guy who remembered everything you'd said to me."

"I liked that nice guy better," I whispered.

"Me too." He nodded.

For the rest of the afternoon and into the evening, we sat at our regular spot by the lake, watching the sun set into the horizon, and talked for hours and hours about everything from our childhood, to our lives after college, to our dreams for the future.

After the sun had set over two hours ago, our conversation had died down, and we sat together, enjoying with comfort the silence of each other's company. Instead of heading home, we continued to sit there in the meadow, lit only by the pale moonlight and the star-filled sky overhead. It was obvious that neither one of us wanted to leave the other—not after we'd finally reconnected again after ten years apart.

As evening completely fell onto the park, a cool breeze blew across the lake and caused a shiver to run down my body.

"Are you cold?" Jackson rubbed his hands up and down my arms, sending more than just warmth through my body.

"Just a little bit," I admitted as I turned to smile at him.

There was a pause before he spoke. "I guess it's getting late, huh?" He took off his blazer and wrapped it over my shoulder.

"Thanks," I whispered as I leaned in to his body for warmth. "Yeah, I guess so," I agreed reluctantly. I didn't want tonight with him to end. I drew in a deep inhale of his intoxicating scent. I never realized before how amazing it was to just be close to him. I could hear his heart pound against his chest as his breathing deepened. We both stared across the lake, the moon's reflection rippling in the water.

Suddenly, I could feel the anticipation in the air as the silence between us continued. I wasn't sure why, but I felt nervous around him.

"Should we walk home now?" he finally asked in a hushed voice.

I turned to face him and we gazed into each other's eyes, seeing only the glow of the moonlight.

Maybe we knew that something had shifted between us at that moment, or maybe we were caught up in this emotionally-charged reunion, or maybe we could no longer deny the unbreakable love between us that went beyond just friendship, but at that moment, it felt as if the world had stilled and stopped around us. As our eyes locked onto one another, everything else faded into the background and before I could think about what was happening, I felt his lips greet mine in a hungry, passionate kiss. With his hands cradling my face, his mouth moved in harmony with mine as we slowly explored each other. A whimper escaped my lips as his tongue parted my mouth and began to taste me. I don't know how long we lost ourselves in the moment, but when we finally pulled out of the kiss, we looked into each other's eyes and just smiled without saying a word.

As the memory of his mouth lingered on my tingling lips, he whispered, almost afraid that speaking any louder would shatter this precious moment, just one word: "Finally."

Chapter Seventeen

Present Day

Thirty Years Old

Jackson

D*ear Chloe,*

Last night seemed like a vivid memory from our childhood, and for the first time in almost a decade, I felt that pure happiness of having you by my side return to me. It was a feeling I'd never thought was possible again. But when I woke up this morning to see you still fast asleep in my arms, I knew what I felt last night had been real, and not a dream. Right now, the sun is just starting to come out over the horizon. It's starting to cast its pale yellow light across your face, and I am in awe with how beautiful and peaceful you look asleep next to me. I'm not sure how I lived without seeing your face for nine years.

As much as I've wanted to resist it, my heart has continued to reach out for you over the years. The hatred I had held onto toward you was built upon the intense hurt and love I've always had for you. Maybe it was fate trying to tell me something, but earlier this week, a quote in the newspaper had caught my eye: "Forgiveness is me giving up my right to hurt you for hurting me." It came at the perfect time. It was right after that night at the wedding reception, that night you'd poured your heart out to me as I sat there ignoring you. And when I went to find you after you ran off in tears, I saw you collapse to the ground and at that moment in time, I thought I might have lost you.

It was then that I'd realized that forgiveness may be the ultimate display of love. And if I truly loved you like I'd always thought I had, then forgiveness was something I had to learn to do.

Please give me time to forgive you, and please also try to forgive me for all the times I've hurt you, forsaken you, and disappointed you. Despite everything that's happened between us, I am choosing to hold onto the moments that my heart cares for the most: the moments I'd fallen in love with you again and again.

Here's to many more of those moments.

Love,

Jackson

I quickly finished the love letter as Chloe was fast asleep next to me in the park. I put the pen and notepad back in her purse. Then I reached over and slipped the note into the front pocket of her jeans. I wanted it to be a surprise, something to put a smile on her face when she'd least expect it. After hearing her recount of the story, I knew I'd wronged her in so many ways, and it was time for me to make up for them, one smile at a time.

"Mmm," Chloe mumbled as she stirred. A few seconds later, her eyes fluttered opened and a sweet smile spread across her face when her eyes focused on me. "Good morning."

"Good morning, sleepyhead. I'm surprised you can sleep with all that noise."

She rubbed her eyes and looked around. "What noise?"

"Your snoring." I shook my head, trying my best to keep my composure. "Why do you think I'm already awake?"

"You're still an ass." She yawned, unfazed by my comment. Even after almost ten years apart, she still knew when I was bluffing. I studied her with amusement as she stretched, trying to wake herself up.

I got up from the grass and looked back at her. "Take my hand." I reached out and offered my hand to her.

She looked at me and cocked an eyebrow. "Should I trust you?"

"You tell me?" I grinned, realizing she remembered our conversation from childhood about what I thought when she would agree to take my hand.

I exaggerated a shrug and placed her hand in mine.

I laughed and pulled her up from the grass. I held her hand as we walked down the pathway. We didn't stop until we reached the small metal bridge on the far end of the lake.

"It's still here," she whispered as she reached for the red heart-shaped love lock that was locked up against the railing. She turned the lock around and her thumb brushed across the inscription etched on the back:

Jax & Clo

June 2003

Unbreakable Friendship & Love.

Promise to Marry in 2014.

"You know," I began. "It's already the beginning of 2015. We're a bit behind."

She turned around to look at me. "Yeah?" She looked at me hopefully.

I nodded.

"But…" she frowned, "where do we even start?"

I pulled her toward me and cupped her face with my hand. I tilted her chin up so I could look straight into her beautiful brown eyes. "Why don't we start from the beginning?"

"The beginning?" She searched my face for an explanation.

"Yes." I beamed down at her. "If you're free tonight, I'd like to take you out to dinner."

She beamed up at me, her cheeks flushed a rosy pink. "You mean like a date?"

I chuckled. "Yes, a real date."

Chapter Eighteen

Present Day

Thirty Years Old

Chloe

"I'm so glad you're okay and coming back home, Aunt Betty." I leaned forward and squeezed her arms over her front passenger seat.

She looked back at me and met my gaze with a warm smile. "Me too, honey. Did Jackson come and talk to you yesterday?"

I couldn't help but smile from ear to ear. "Yeah, he did. I know it's going to take some time for us to truly forgive everything that we've done to each other, whether intentional or not, but I think we both want to work it out and move past it."

"Oh, that's so great, honey." She placed her hand to her chest. "I'm so happy for you."

I beamed. "Me too. I really can't believe it, actually. He's actually taking me out on our first date tonight."

"Wow, I can't believe it took that boy twenty-three years to build up the courage to ask you out."

"Uncle Tom!" I giggled. "You're so mean."

Uncle Tom raised his hands in the air. "Hey, not mean. Wise. Don't you remember? I called it that very first day you moved in with us that he was teasing you because he liked you."

"He actually did," Aunt Betty nodded with a laugh. "Well, honey, that'll be a fun time. What are you guys planning on doing?"

"I'm not sure, actually. He said he'd surprise me."

"Awww. How sweet."

"Yeah." For the rest of the car ride home from the hospital, I couldn't help but daydream about what our first date would be like.

While Uncle Tom helped Aunt Betty into the house when we pulled up, I opened the trunk to grab Aunt Betty's things. Since she'd stayed for a few days, Uncle Tom had brought her a box of her scrapbooking items to help her days go faster.

"Aunt Betty, where would you like me to put your scrapbooking stuff?" I called out as I walked through the front hallway.

"Can you put the actual scrapbook on the bookshelf in the study, and you can take the box of scrapbooking supplies up into the attic for now."

"You got it."

"Thanks, honey."

When I got up to the attic, I realized that I'd never been up here before. I was surprised to see how many boxes of things that were stored up here. I even noticed a few boxes with my name on them.

As I was riffling through some of the boxes of my things from childhood, I noticed a few boxes tucked farther into the attic that caught my eye. From the darker age-worn shade of the boxes and the thick layers of dust that seemed to blanket them, they seemed to have been untouched for decades.

My curiosity got the best of me as I pushed through the dozen of boxes that came between me and the old cluster of boxes. When I made it to them, I brushed aside some of the dust to see what was written on the boxes.

Judy's Stuff

I gasped seeing my mom's name on a few of the boxes. These boxes contained my mom's things. I'd never really seen any of her things before and had no idea they'd been stored here this entire time. I opened one of the boxes. It contained mostly clothes. I dug through the box and underneath some clothes was a large ruby-colored jewelry box. I picked up the box, feeling the rich velvet beneath my fingers.

When I opened the box, my eyes lit up to see it filled with stacks and stacks of letters addressed to my mom.

As I flipped through some of the letters, I realized they looked like love letters, all written in the same handwriting.

My mind whirled at this discovery and as much as I didn't want to hope it to be true, my thoughts instantly wondered if these letters could be from my father—the mystery man my mom had never talked about, even before her drinking completely took over her life.

Suddenly one letter caught my attention.

Judy,

That night we first met in front of your sister's house when you were getting her mail, I knew it was fate that had brought us together. After talking to you for those few magical minutes, I knew there was something undeniably real between us. You mentioned that night how much you love writing and receiving handwritten letters, so here is the beginning of my love letters to you.

Love,

John

Then I caught my name mentioned in another letter.

Judy,

You are the world to me, my love. You know that, right? Then you should know how happy I was when you told me that you were pregnant with our child. And only you would be so prepared to be a mother that you've already decided on what you'd want to name your first born. Chloe and Jeffrey are perfect names!

It makes me sad that you were worried at first about telling me. You should know me by now, and you should know that nothing would make me happier than to start a family with you and grow old with you. Don't worry about my parents. They will eventually come around and realize how perfect you are for me. Once I have things figured out with them, I want you to marry me! I hope you say yes, my love.

Always Yours,

John

I stared at the letter, overwhelmed with emotion. *They're talking about me before I was born!*

My mom had said that my father had passed away before I was born. But was it possible that he was still alive? It sounded like the guy's parents didn't approve of his relationship with my mom. *Was this why my mom didn't tell me about him? Could this be my father?*

I flipped through the stash of letters and finally found one of the original envelopes that came with one of the letters. When I turned the envelope around and saw the name on the return address, my body froze as I felt all the oxygen being sucked out of the room. Shock flooded my entire body, numbing everything in its path.

John Pierce.

Jackson's father. The man I had slept with. The man who'd once loved my mom.

My knees suddenly gave out and I collapsed onto the floor as the weight of what this all meant became too heavy to bear.

Could Jackson's father be my *father? Could Jackson and I actually be half brothers and sisters?* And then another sickening thought caused my stomach to twist in unease. *Had I really slept with my own father?*

Panic gripped me and I found it difficult to breathe. "This can't be true," I cried as I shook my head. "This just can't!" I stared at the letter in utter disbelief.

Unable to accept this reality, I felt an uncontrollable urge to run away from everything.

Without a word, I left the house and got into my car. I wasn't sure where I was going, but I wanted to be anywhere but here. I pulled out of the driveway and sped off down the street.

Tears streamed down my eyes as I tried to process what this all could mean. Feeling frantic and out of control, my foot pressed farther down onto the gas pedal.

Suddenly, before I knew that it was happening, I watched in surprise as my car flew off the edge of the bridge. As if in slow motion, the world started spinning outside my car window, and the sickening sensation of falling at high speed gripped the pit of my stomach. Before the impact of the water hit the car, the last thing I registered was the empty darkness that engulfed me.

Author's Note

Thank you for reading *Promise to Keep*, book two in the three-book series *Promises*. The unforgettable conclusion to Chloe and Jackson's story unfolds in *Promise of Forever* which will be out on March 31, 2015 and available on pre-order.

Please also consider telling your friends about and leaving a review for this book. As an indie author, word of mouth and reviews help other readers to discovery my works.

Other Books

If you would like to stay informed of new releases, teasers, and news on my upcoming books, please sign up for Jessica Wood's mailing list or visit me at my website:

http://jessicawoodauthor.com/mailing-list/

http://jessicawoodauthor.com

Below is a list of Jessica Wood's books:

Emma's Story Series
- *A Night to Forget* – Book One
- *The Day to Remember* – Book Two
- *Emma's Story* Box Set – Contains Book One & Book Two

The Heartbreaker Series

This is an *Emma's Story* spin-off series featuring Damian Castillo, a supporting character in *The Day to Remember*. This is a standalone series and does not need to be read with *Emma's Story* series.

- *Damian* – Book One
- *The Heartbreaker* – Prequel Novella to *DAMIAN* – can be read before or after *Damian*.
- *Taming Damian* – Book Two
- *The Heartbreaker Box Set* – Contains all three books.

The Chase Series

This is a standalone series with cameo appearances from Damian Castillo (*The Heartbreaker series*).

- *The Chase, Vol. 1*
- *The Chase, Vol. 2*
- *The Chase, Vol. 3*
- *The Chase, Vol. 4*
- *The Chase: The Complete Series Box Set* – Contains All Four Volumes

Oblivion

This is a standalone full-length book unrelated to other series by Jessica Wood.

- *Oblivion*

Promises Series

This is a standalone series unrelated to other series by Jessica Wood.

Promise to Marry – Book One

Promise to Keep – Book Two

Promise of Forever – Book Three

***

Oblivion – Synopsis & Excerpt

SYNOPSIS

I wake up to a life and a man that I can't remember.

He says his name is Connor Brady—the tall, sexy CEO of Brady Global, Inc.

He says my name is Olivia Stuart, and that I was recently in an accident and lost my memory.

Also, he says I'm his fiancé.

Although I don't remember Connor, or anything about my past, something about him seems familiar. He is kind, protective, and breathtakingly-gorgeous. But there is just one problem—he seems *too* perfect.

As I begin to rebuild my relationship with Connor and accept the idea that I may never remember my past, I unexpectedly meet Ethan James.

Ethan is the mysterious, rebellious stranger who pushes my boundaries to their limits and makes me feel alive. As our lives collide time and time again, the bits and pieces of my past start to unravel, unearthing the secrets that have been buried deep inside my subconscious. With every new memory I gain about who I once was, I become more torn between the man who is my fiancé and the stranger who is the key to my past. Is my life with Connor really as perfect as he leads me to believe?

CHAPTER ONE

Tears streamed down my face as I ran into my bedroom and slammed the door behind me. I reached for my diary—the familiar pink leather journal that was filled with my deepest thoughts. My shaky fingers pulled the gold fabric ribbon page marker, taking me to my last entry, and I began to frantically scribble down everything I was feeling at that moment—all the pain and fear that raced inside me as the screaming escalated an octave higher between my parents outside of my room.

They're fighting again. It's been happening more and more frequently, each time worse than the day before.

I wish they weren't so unhappy. I wish my parents didn't hate each other so much. I wish I was anyone else but myself right now. I wish I was anywhere else but here.

As if hearing my thoughts, I heard my father roar, "If you want a fucking divorce, you can have it! But I'm going to warn you just this once: if you walk out of that door, don't ever think about coming back again!"

"I don't plan on it!" I heard my mother spit back. "I'm leaving first thing tomorrow, and I'm taking Liv with me!"

"No!" I cried, my mind racing as I thought about everything I was about to lose.

Just then, my room and the pink leather diary in my hand faded away into the background as my consciousness registered a soft, steady beeping in the distance. What is that?

When I turned toward the sound, I found myself running across a familiar street in the middle of the night. I was wearing a jewel-encrusted blush-pink evening gown that weighed down on my body and restricted my movement. The air was bitter cold and cutting, but the adrenaline that coursed inside me seemed to shelter me from the cold like a numbing blanket.

Suddenly, I saw two bright, blinding headlights coming toward me at high speed. The sharp screeching of car tires filled the air, drowning out all other noise. I felt the impact of cold metal against my body as I was lifelessly flung sideways against the solid pavement.

I braced myself for the impact of the pain that would greet my body.

But it didn't come.

Instead, the steady beeping returned, but this time, it seemed closer, louder.

Then a hushed conversation seeped through my consciousness.

"There's nothing we can do for her right now, Mr. Brady. As you know she has suffered some head injuries from the accident, so all we can do right now is to wait for her to wake up and see from there." The female voice seemed miles away, but for some reason, I knew she was talking about me.

"Okay. Thank you." The man's voice was strained and low as I heard him walk in my direction.

I felt my head throb in pain, in time with that unnerving beeping that became increasingly louder.

"She's very lucky to have someone like you to visit and be by her side every day. You must really care about her."

"Yeah. I do." The male voice was closer than before.

Then I felt a warm hand on mine, bringing me into the present. My mind registered the bed I was lying on. The smell of stale, chlorine air invaded my senses. The beeping came into focus and I could hear it coming from a machine a foot away from me. *Am I in a hospital?*

My fingers twitched as I tried to move my body.

"Nurse!" the man's voice cried out in alarm. "I think I felt her move."

My eyes fluttered open and closed, struggling against the heaviness of my lids and the blinding lights that stung my eyes.

"I think she's waking up!" The man squeezed my hand as he inched closer to my face. "Liv?"

"Mr. Brady, let's give her some room." The man loosened his grip on me and I heard him move away.

I opened my eyes again, and this time, it was easier. My vision was blurred as I looked around, but I could detect two figures close by.

"Ms. Stuart?" The female voice was gentle as she moved toward me.

"Where am I?" I blinked and after a couple of seconds, her face came into focus. "Who are you?" I looked around the room and found myself in a surprisingly large and luxurious hospital room.

"Ms. Stuart, you were in an accident and you're at The Pavilion, a private in-patient hospital unit at the University of Pennsylvania hospital. I'm Nurse Betty and I've been taking care of you."

"An accident." I repeated her words and tried to think through the dense fog consuming my every thought. Then I winced at the throbbing pain in my head.

"Are you in any pain?" She looked at me with concern.

"Just a horrible headache." I reached for my head.

"I'll let the doctor know and we'll get you something for that."

"What happened to me?" I looked up at her, searching her face for answers.

She flashed me a kind smile. "There's actually someone that's been here waiting for you to wake up for quite some time. I'll let him tell you what happened while I check your vitals." She moved aside and my eyes focused on the other figure in the room—the tall, handsome man in a tailored charcoal suit standing anxiously behind her.

"Hi." I looked at him, unsure of what else to say to this stranger.

"Liv? Thank God you finally woke up."

I smiled at him. His warm, hazel eyes were filled with concern as he moved in front of the nurse to grab my hand. I studied him, wondering why he seemed so familiar.

He reached for me. Deep creases formed between his brows as he furrowed them in worry. "Liv, how are you feeling?" His voice was smooth and gentle. I couldn't quite place where, but I knew I'd heard it before.

I placed my hands to my head and groaned. "Besides this killer headache, I'm okay." I tried to get up but my arms felt weak as I slumped back down against the pillows when I tried to sit up. He reached over and helped me lean up against the headboard of the bed.

"It's so good to see you awake." He held my face and kissed me gently on my forehead.

I flinched and frowned up at him. "Who are you? Have we met before?"

His expression changed immediately and he whipped around and turned to the nurse. I saw them exchange a look that I didn't understand.

He then turned back to me and frowned, his eyes filled with sadness. "You don't remember me?"

I studied his face and thought about it. "No, I don't think so," I finally said as I shook my head.

"What's the last thing you remember?" he asked me tentatively. I didn't need to know this man to detect the anxious expression on his face.

I stared at him and tried to rack my brain, searching for anything I could remember. I shook my head in frustration as I buried it in my hands. My head was pounding in pain as if I had just awoken from the worst hangover of my life.

"Liv, are you okay? What's wrong?" The alarm in his voice exacerbated the panic that was building inside.

"Why do you keep calling me Liv?" I felt annoyed as I looked back up at him. My annoyance turned to worry when I saw the shocked expression on his face.

The nurse stepped forward. "Do you remember your name?"

I opened my mouth, ready to answer her simple question, but then stopped. It was only then, when I was forced to think about it, that it dawned on me that I didn't actually know the answer. "I...I can't remember."

"Is there anything you do remember?" Her tone was gentle and cautious.

I searched my thoughts, trying to grab onto any memory. But everything outside the last few minutes seemed like a dream that I had somehow forgotten the moment I woke up. *Why can't I remember anything?* I shook my head in frustration. "What happened to me?"

"I'll let Mr. Brady here tell you what happened while I go get Dr. Miller."

"Honey, I'm Connor. Connor Brady. Are you sure you don't remember me?" The man moved back toward me, a mixture of hopefulness and uncertainty painted across his face.

"Connor," I repeated in a monotone voice. I studied him, trying to place him to some moment in my life. There was something about him that was familiar, but as hard as I tried, I couldn't seem to remember how I knew him. I shook my head slowly. "I don't even remember my own name."

"Your name is Olivia Stuart. Your friends call you Liv." He sat down on the chair next to my bed and placed his hand on top of mine. His hand was warm and familiar but it felt weird to have this stranger touching me in this intimate way. I didn't pull my hand away, though. I needed answers and this man seemed to have them, so the last thing I wanted to do was to offend him.

"What happened to me?"

His face fell. "You were in a hit-and-run accident." His voice cracked and he cleared his throat. He paused before continuing. "You've been in a coma for the past eight days since the accident."

Panic and confusion swirled around me at the idea of losing so much time without knowing it. "Eight days? But…but I don't remember any of this. Why can't I remember anything?" I felt frantic as I tried to push through the fog and my mind came back blank.

"Liv, you sustained some head injuries from the accident. The doctors said that memory loss was a possibility when you woke up…"

I stared at him in disbelief as my hands immediately moved up to my head. When my fingers traced the layers of bandages, I knew he was telling me the truth.

"Don't worry. The doctors say that if there's memory loss, it might only be temporary," he tried to reassure me. "You might slowly regain your memories back."

"Might?" I didn't feel reassured by that word.

Just then a middle-aged bald man in a white lab coat walked into the room. A warm smile appeared on his friendly face. "Ms. Stuart. I'm Dr. Miller. It's great to see you awake. How are you feeling?"

"What's wrong with me, Dr. Miller? Why can't I remember who I am?"

"Let me ask you a few questions first, alright?"

"Okay."

"Do you know when you were born?"

I searched my mind, trying to recall the answer. Nothing. I shook my head.

"Do you know where you went to high school?"

"No." I shook my head again as I felt the frustration and helplessness grow inside.

"Do you know the name of Philadelphia's football team?"

To my surprise, I didn't draw a blank this time. "The Eagles."

"You remember," Connor said excitedly as he squeezed my hand.

Dr. Miller smiled. "Can you tell me how many states there are in the U.S.?"

"Fifty." I frowned at the doctor, wondering if that was a trick question. "There are a few territories like Puerto Rico and Guam though," I added.

"Well, it looks like you've suffered from some memory loss due to the accident, but not all. It's not uncommon for someone to have some degree of amnesia after a traumatic event like the one you experienced. From your answers, it appears the amnesia has affected your episodic memory, which is the memory of experiences and specific events—the memories personal to you. But it seems that the amnesia didn't affect your semantic memory, which is the memory dealing with facts and your knowledge of the eternal world." He studied the clipboard in his hands. "The good news is from all the tests we've run on you, it doesn't seem like there was any damage to the areas of your brain that store your long-term memories."

"What does that mean, doctor?" the handsome man in the charcoal suit cut in to ask.

"Well it should mean that Ms. Stuart hasn't suffered any long-term memory loss."

"So I don't understand. Why can't I remember anything about myself, then?"

"That's the thing we don't know at this time. The brain is a miraculous and mysterious thing. It's unlikely that you're suffering from any permanent brain damage."

"So what's the problem?" Connor asked, his grip tightened around my hand.

"Sometimes the brain will suppress memories after going through a traumatic experience. That memory hasn't been forgotten in the traditional sense, but it's locked away by the sub-conscious and removed from the conscious mind."

"So does that mean I'll get my memories back?" I looked at him hopefully.

"The chances are good, but it's also not a guarantee either that you'll get some or all of your memories back. The best thing for you is to go back to your life before the accident and surround yourself with the things that are familiar and important to you—those are usually the things that will help trigger your memories."

"Liv, baby, I promise to help you through this." Connor held up my hand between both of his as he pulled it close to his chest. He looked up at Dr. Miller. "Doc, what's the next step?"

"Well Ms. Stuart, since you just woke up from the coma, I'd like to run some tests and keep you under careful observation at the hospital for a week or so. During this time, you'll also start your physical therapy to strengthen your muscles that have been inactive while you've been here. If the tests look good, then we can have you released as early as next week."

"Thank you, doctor. That's good news." Connor beamed at me.

But as much as I tried, I couldn't seem to adopt his excitement.

Sensing my unease, his expression changed. "What's wrong, honey?"

As if taking this as a signal, the doctor cleared his throat. "Ms. Stuart, we'll let you guys talk. I'll check up on you in an hour or so to run those tests."

Anxiety built inside me as I watched the doctor and nurse slip out of the room. Even though I knew that this man in the charcoal suit seemed to know who I was, he still felt like a stranger to me, and being completely alone with him made me uneasy.

"What are you thinking, Liv?" he finally broke the silence.

"Liv...Olivia." I said my name aloud. It sounded foreign, yet familiar from my mouth. I then met

Connor's gaze. He smiled at me as he studied my expression. "I still don't know who you are exactly. I mean, I know your name is Connor, but…how do we know each other?"

His smile disappeared and I saw the sadness in his eyes again. "Liv, I'm your fiancé."

"Fiancé?"

He nodded. I followed his gaze as it darted down to my left hand. To my surprise, there on my ring finger was a large, sparkling diamond set on top of a platinum, diamond-encrusted eternity band. *How did I not see this earlier?*

I looked back at him in silence, overwhelmed by everything.

"This must be a lot for you to take in right now. And I'm sure you have a lot of questions. I'll be happy to answer whatever I know. Let's just take this one step at a time. We can go at the pace you're most comfortable with, okay?"

I nodded and drew in a deep breath as thousands of questions whirled around in my head, fighting for my attention.

"Thanks." I gave him a small smile, grateful for his patience and understanding. At that moment I thought about how hard this must be for him as well—to be engaged to and in love with someone who doesn't remember you or feel that same love anymore.

"Can we take this slowly? I just feel really overwhelmed."

"Of course, Liv. I understand. Whatever you need. Just tell me what you want. Okay?"

I nodded again. "Who are my parents? Do I have any siblings? Do they know I'm here?"

I saw the pained expression on Connor's face and knew I wouldn't like the answer.

"I'm sorry, Liv. Your mom passed away a few years ago. You don't have any siblings."

"Did you know my mom? What kind of person was she?" Tears streamed down my face as I felt the loss for the mother I couldn't remember.

"She passed away right before we met here in Philly. I believe you left New Jersey and moved here to start a new life."

"Oh. And my dad?"

He shook his head. "You rarely talked about him. From the little you have said, you haven't seen him since you were thirteen—"

"—when my parents got a divorce…" I finished his comment as I remembered the flashback I had right before I woke up.

"Yeah." Connor looked at me in alarm. "Are you remembering things?"

"Maybe. I had a flashback of them fighting when I was young right before I woke up."

"Oh. Did you get any other flashbacks?"

"I don't know. I think a little bit from the accident."

"Oh?"

"Yeah. I think I was running across the street and then a car came toward me and hit me."

"I'm so sorry, Liv." Connor buried his face in his hands. "It's all my fault."

"What do you mean? Were you driving that car?" I looked at him in alarm.

"No, of course not!" He shook his head. "I...I just feel responsible for you."

I frowned. I could tell there was something he wasn't telling me. "Do you know how my accident happened? Were you there?"

He nodded and looked away. "I wish I could take it all back. I wish..."

"What happened? Please tell me."

He looked up at me and I saw the regret in his face. "It was the night of our engagement party at the Franklin Institute Science Museum." His eyes glazed over and he smiled as his thoughts took him back to that night. "You looked absolutely gorgeous in that jeweled gown." He paused and his expression turned somber. "At some point during the night, you went out to the front of the museum. That's when the car hit you."

"I remember running across the street when the car hit me," I said slowly as I thought back to the flashback I had right before I woke up. I stared at him, trying to remember more from that night. *How come it's so hard to remember?* I thought in frustration.

"I'm so sorry, Liv. I should have been there for you. Maybe if I were there, this wouldn't have happened…"

I frowned, trying to figure out how to comfort this man who seemed to be consumed with guilt. "You didn't know this was going to happen." I saw the anguish in his eyes and reached for his hand to reassure him. "It's not your fault."

"But it did happen." I saw his body stiffen and knew it wasn't going to be easy for him to forgive himself.

"Connor, please don't."

He looked up at me with pained eyes.

"There's nothing you could've done differently when you didn't know. I wish I had my memories. I wish I hadn't been running across the street when the car came. I wish things were different." I blinked away a tear. "But sometimes we don't always get what we wish for. Sometimes we can only work with the hand that we're dealt." I was surprised by the sudden acceptance I felt for what had happened. *Maybe those who say, "ignorance is bliss," are right.*

"Is there anything I can do to help?"

I looked at this stranger and somehow I knew I would remember him again. I knew he was important to me. I looked down at the engagement ring on my finger and instantly felt a loss for all the special memories that I didn't have anymore.

"What's wrong, Liv?" He saw the fresh tears in my eyes that were threatening to make their way down my cheeks.

"It's just a lot to take in all at once."

"I know."

I watched him gently brush the tears from my cheeks, and from the way his hands caressed my face, I knew he'd touched me many times before. *Were we happy before this accident? What kind of person was I when we were together? What did I enjoy doing?* It wasn't until then that another question hit me like a ton of bricks. *What do I look like?*

I gave him a weak smile. "Connor, I'm really tired. I'd like some time alone to digest all this."

His brows furrowed with worry but he didn't try to object. "Okay." He got up from the chair and looked down at me. "I'll stop by first thing tomorrow morning to see you."

"Okay." I forced a small smile.

He leaned down toward me and kissed me gently on my forehead. "I'll see you tomorrow. I love you, gorgeous," he whispered.

As I watched him leave, the hospital room suddenly disappeared.

For a split second I found myself in a grand, sun-drenched bedroom lying naked on a large luxurious bed under lush layers of satin sheets. I screamed out and my back arched upward as intense pleasure radiated throughout my body. I felt a pair of strong, rough hands grip my thighs tightly, keeping them spread apart as a long and hard tongue plunged in and out of me, pushing me to the brink of my release. After I came, I felt another naked body move up my body from somewhere under the layers and a second later, Connor's face emerged out from under the sheets. He flashed me a wicked smirk as he slowly licked his lips. "And that's how much I love you, gorgeous."

I gasped at the memory that had just hit me, and my body tingled as if that moment had just happened. I looked down at my body and the question that had blindsided me a few minutes earlier crossed my mind again. *What do I look like?*

I slowly got up from the bed, and felt my muscles weak from the days of being on the hospital bed. It took me several minutes to move to the bathroom where there was a full-length mirror along the wall facing the door.

Standing in front of the mirror was like standing face to face with a complete stranger. Nerves prickled through my body like ice, cold needles as I studied every inch of the unfamiliar person in front of me. Nothing about my reflection looked familiar. Her radiant blue eyes stared back at me. Even through the bandages around her forehead, I could see the long wavy blond hair that cascaded down the curves of her small frame. I watched as this stunning woman staring back at me touched her face with both hands. I felt her fingers move across my face.

"I'm Olivia Stuart." My whispered words filled the silent room and seemed to hang in the air as I continued to study myself in the reflection. *Will this ever stop feeling so strange?*

***

After a week at the hospital and focusing on my physical therapy, I felt slightly better and hopeful about everything. The tests Dr. Miller had ran all came out normal and I was cleared to leave today.

"Hey, gorgeous."

I looked up to find Connor at my door with a large bouquet of pink roses.

"Hi." I smiled, happy to see a familiar face. "You're back."

"Of course I'm back, silly. I've been visiting you every day, and every day you seem surprised to see me. Are you trying to get rid of me or something?"

I could see from his smile that he was joking, and I giggled uneasily. "No, that's not what I mean." I wasn't sure how to tell him that the reason I seemed surprised to see him was because to me, he felt like a stranger.

"Well, like it or not, I'm here to take you home today, like I'd promised."

"Oh, right." Our eyes met and I felt my stomach flip nervously. I immediately looked away and felt my face turn beet red when I remembered my flashback of the intense orgasm this man had given me. I knew that for him, we were lovers in love, but for me, I felt embarrassed and exposed that this handsome stranger knew me more intimately than I knew myself.

"What's wrong?" He walked over to me and kissed me lightly on my cheek.

"Nothing." I pushed my thoughts aside and flashed him a smile.

He handed me the bouquet in his hands. "Pink roses are your favorite."

"Thank you. They're beautiful." I took the stunning bouquet and was instantly hit with its intoxicating smell.

"How are you feeling?"

"Better," I responded honestly.

"Good. So are you ready to blow this popsicle stand then?"

I let out a light chuckle and nodded.

Thirty minutes later, Connor had helped me finish all my paperwork to check out of the hospital. I had changed into a white Splendid cotton silk tee, dark-washed J Brand jeans, and a pair of black Christian Louboutin patent leather stilettos that Connor brought for me from my closet. According to him, this was one of my favorite casual outfits. I had stared dubiously at the three-inch heels when he had handed them to me. They looked more painful than comfortable to me. But when I put them on, they had hugged my feet perfectly and I was surprised by how at ease I was walking around in them.

"Hey, gorgeous." Connor looked up from the hospital paperwork when I walked out of the bathroom. "You look like you're back to your old self." I watched as his eyes moved up and down my body, and a nervous shiver ran down my back.

"I guess my muscle memory's still intact," I joked as I looked at my heels.

He chuckled and shook his head. "I never did understand how you could walk in those things. You know on one of our first dates, I called you Wonder Woman when I saw you running in a pair just like those."

I smiled. "Why was I running?"

"We had just had an amazing date at Tria, this great wine bar in the city, and you had a few glasses too many." He smiled as he told the story. "Well, by the end of the night, you were running and skipping down the street without a care in the world and giggling uncontrollably." He laughed at the memory and beamed at me. "It was at that moment that I knew I'd fall in love with you."

I laughed along with him, wishing I could remember that memory, wishing I could remember how it had felt to possibly share those same feelings toward him.

A few minutes later we were outside, standing at the entrance of the hospital.

"Liv, I'm going to go get the car. You okay with waiting right here for me? I'll bring the car around and pick you up."

I nodded and smiled. He's such a gentleman.

He leaned in and kissed me gently on the forehead. "I love you, gorgeous."

"Thanks." I cringed inside as soon as the word came out. I wasn't sure what to say. I had a feeling he wanted more, but telling a stranger I loved him wasn't something I was ready to give.

He gave a light chuckle and smiled. "I'll be back."

As I watched him walk away and turn the corner toward the entrance of the parking garage, I was preoccupied with thoughts of how the following days, weeks, and months would be for us.

Suddenly I heard people approach me from the left.

"Excuse me! Please make way!"

I turned and saw a couple barreling toward me. It was a man holding up a pregnant woman who appeared to be in a lot of pain. "My wife's water broke! Please move!"

I finally realized that I was standing in the middle of the hospital entrance and blocking their path. I hastily took a step back to give them room to pass me, but it was too late. The man pushed past me and as I took a step back, my heel caught on a crack in the pavement and I lost my balance and fell backward.

Just as I thought I was about to hit the ground, a strong arm caught me from behind and pulled me up. I gasped in surprise at my near-fall and found myself tightly clutched within someone's protective arms.

"Careful there or you're going to hurt yourself in those killer heels."

I looked up and let out an audible gasp as my gaze locked with a pair of intensely-dark, smoldering brown eyes staring down at me.

If you enjoyed this excerpt from *Oblivion*, a completely standalone full-length book, the book is currently available.

About the Author

Jessica Wood writes new adult contemporary romance.

While she has lived in countless cities throughout the U.S., her heart belongs to San Francisco. To her, there's something seductively romantic about the Golden Gate Bridge, the steep rolling hills of the city streets, the cable cars, and the Victorian-style architecture.

Jessica loves a strong, masculine man with a witty personality. While she is headstrong and stubbornly independent, she can't resist a man who takes control of the relationship, both outside and inside of the bedroom.

She loves to travel internationally, and tries to plan a yearly trip abroad. She also loves to cook and bake, and—to the benefit of her friends—she loves to share. She also enjoys ceramics and being creative with her hands. She has a weakness for good (maybe bad) TV shows; she's up-to-date on over 25 current shows, and no, that wasn't a joke.

And it goes without saying, she loves books—they're like old and dear friends who have always been there to make her laugh and make her cry.

The one thing she wished she had more of is time.

If you would like to follow or contact Jessica Wood, you can do so through the following:

Mailing List: http://jessicawoodauthor.com/mailing-list/

Blog: http://jessicawoodauthor.com

Facebook: www.facebook.com/jessicawoodauthor

Twitter: http://twitter.com/jesswoodauthor

Pinterest: http://pinterest.com/jessicawooda/

Printed in Great Britain
by Amazon.co.uk, Ltd.,
Marston Gate.